PF

SEÁN

WEEPING SEASON

"Fast, thrilling, and brutal, *Weeping Season* leaves you gasping for breath. O'Connor's prose is sharp and lean, and he has a great eye for the grisly. Thoroughly recommended."

—TIM LEBBON
New York Times bestselling author of the *Relics trilogy*

"Vivid, unflinching, evocative, and original, O'Connor's work heralds the arrival of an important voice in horror fiction, one to which you would do well to listen."

—KEALAN PATRICK BURKE
Bram Stoker Award-winning author of *The Turtle Boy*,
KIN, and *Sour Candy*

"O'Connor's imagination knows no limits. A standout new voice in horror fiction."

—MATT HAYWARD
Bram Stoker Award-nominated author of
What Do Monsters Fear?

"A fast-paced read you'll devour in one or two sittings. The action and horrors are relentless, and you'll never see the ending coming. Bleak, terrifying, and thoroughly entertaining."

—PHILIP FRACASSI
This Is Horror Award-winning Author of
Behold the Void

"O'Connor has a knack for writing a narrative that is so smooth and fluid, I forget that I'm reading and not watching. There were scenes in this book that terrified me to my core."

—★★★★★
SADIE HARTMANN
NightWorms Review / Cemetery Dance / Scream Magazine

"Seán O'Connor's Weeping Season grips the reader in madness and uncertainty from page one and never let's go. A sinister mystery unfolding fast and hard in the woods, a group of scared, wounded people left with nothing but fragments of memory, Weeping Season gets under your skin like a chill and carries you along in its icy tide. Read it and shiver."

—MARY SANGIOVANNI
Bram Stoker Award nominee
& author of *Behind The Door*

"Seán O'Connor presents *Weeping Season*, a novel drawn from the same realm as *Black Mirror* and *The Outer Limits*, but with a brutality normally reserved for the Splatterpunk genre. *Weeping Season* functions as an adult exploration of what exactly it means to be human and humane in the face of uncompromising and brutal cruelty. For a generation of teens raised on the likes of *The Hunger Games*, *Weeping Season* returns to familiar territory but with a wicked sensibility reserved for mature readers."

—PETER RAWLIK
Author of *The Peaslee Papers: A Lovecraftian Chronicle*

"A completely engaging and unique read that left me wanting."

—★★★★★
TRACY ROBINSON
SciFiAndScary.com

"Frankly, I wasn't sure if there would be a resolution satisfying enough for the brisk and horrific mystery O'Connor was leading toward, but happily I was wrong."

—★★★★
MICHAEL PATRICK HICKS
High Fever Books Review

"A chilling piece of Dark Fiction. *Black Mirror* fans rejoice."

—★★★★★
DUBLIN GAZETTE

"O'Connor's writing appeals to me a great deal — entwined with the more straightforward style was attractive prose and poetic flourishes. I want to read more from this author because I sincerely believe in his potential."

—CATHERINE FLORENCE
Red Lace Reviews

"*Weeping Season* is a vivid, wicked and wholly engaging read, filled with distinct characters and cringe-worthy scenes worthy of any horror fans' shelves."

—ALEX J. KNUDSON
Author of *The Nawie*

"Fast, creepy, tense and has some amazing character building. This is a no-brainer five star debut that acts as a reminder of the continuous stream of literary talent Ireland has to offer."

—★★★★★
GINGER NUTS OF HORROR

WEEPING SEASON

Also by Seán O'Connor

The Mongrel

January 14th, 2020

Dear Marie,
   Can't wait to hear you talk about this one...

The WEEPING SEASON

has begun...

SEÁN O'CONNOR

UAFÁS
PRESS

"I'm Forever Blowing Bubbles"
Lyrics by John Kellette © Copyright 1919
Free to use under the Duration of Copyright Act 2004

Grateful acknowledgement is made to Pallbearer
for permission to reprint an excerpt from "Worlds Apart"
Lyrics and music by Pallbearer © Copyright 2014

Grateful acknowledgement is made to Patrick Walker
for permission to reprint an excerpt from "Footprints" by Warning
Lyrics and music by Patrick Walker © Copyright 2006

Typeset in 11pt Bookman Old Style & interior design by Kenneth W.
Cain

Cover artwork & external design by Boz Mugabe

Uafás Press
Dublin, Ireland

Legal Deposit and Library Cataloguing in Publication Data.
A catalogue record for this book is available from The National Library
of Ireland.

ISBN: 978-1-5272-5448-0

For Raymond & Sandra

"Without dark
The light burns out our eyes
And turns each of us to ash
Our hearts, too hard to ever learn to feel
And mouths, laid open, deep in silent song"
—PALLBEARER, "Worlds Part"

"And through all the battles around me
I never believed I would fight;
Yet here I stand, a broken soldier,
Shivering, naked, in your winter light."
—WARNING, "Footprints"

AWAKENING

ONE

Aman awoke to hysterical screams. Cold dirt pressed against his cheek as he blinked to clear his vision. When he lifted his head and looked up, an awning of pine branches swayed overhead. He grappled to catch his bearings as he pushed up to sit, stiff all over, hard shivers running through him. Then it dawned on him that he was naked and covered in muck, his body as cold as the freezing surface he sat on. When he went to move, pain shot up his left leg, bringing his attention to a manacle around his ankle, a solid-looking chain running from it to a thick pine tree that soared up to the heavens.

A short distance away, a young girl howled and battled against the heavy steel that secured her to another tree. Her cries echoed through his head as he tried to focus, continuing to blink away the blurred edges of his vision. What was going on? Where the hell were they? Acknowledging her distress, he went to stand but couldn't find the strength to complete the action, collapsing to the ground, drained of energy, with every part of him in pain.

Water, he needed water. His tongue and throat were parched. He licked his lips, or tried to, wincing at the resulting sting. Both were chapped and bone dry. Black clay was embedded beneath his fingernails, which came as no surprise considering the dirt that covered him. He tried to call to the girl, but no words came, just a racking cough that tore through his chest and head. The chill from the frozen ground was too much and he pressed his fists into the dirt and forced himself up – his weak arms barely carrying his bodyweight.

"Hey," he called to her, glad to be able to vocalise.

She didn't seem to hear him, continuing with her struggle.

"Hey, what's going on?" he shouted, looking around, his voice hollow across the forest floor.

This time she stopped and turned to him.

"I thought you were...dead." Her voiced sounded as dry and tortured as his. "I was calling to you for ages."

He took another look around. "Where are we?"

She didn't answer, returning to her efforts to break loose from her bonds.

He watched her struggle. She was so petite, he supposed she couldn't have been much older than her mid-twenties, but to his eyes she was like a girl of fifteen or sixteen, which made his looking at her naked body feel somewhat inappropriate. He figured he was old enough to be her father. Before he looked away, he noticed her head had been shaved and she had the figure eight tattooed in black just above the hairline at the back. From where he stood, it looked fresh, with dried blood on and around it.

What was going on? This was such a crazy situation. The chain that held him to the tree was thick and made of heavy steel. His legs trembled, barely able to hold him, but the ground was too cold to sit or lie on. Dense forest lay in every direction, with weak light filtering through tiny gaps in the canopy. No sun to melt the frost. How had they got here? The girl started crying again as she pulled at her chain.

"Hey now. Calm down for a second."

She ignored him, struggling on until she ran out of energy and slumped against the tree in defeat. While wiping tears from her filthy face, she kept muttering the same words to herself: "Why is this happening to me?"

"What's your name?" he asked. "Come on, talk to me here."

"I don't know my name," she barked back. "I don't know anything."

It was at that point it dawned on him that he didn't know his own name, either. He searched, scanning every thought or visual that came to him, realising with a growing horror that he didn't know anything from before wakening to her screams.

Everything before was blank. But how? What could have happened? There had to be a rational explanation. They couldn't have just appeared here out of nowhere. It wasn't possible. Was it?

"What can you remember?" he asked her, making a conscious effort to keep the panic out of his voice. "Come on, think about it. You have to remember something."

"Nothing." She slapped her bald head with both hands, growling out her frustration. "Fucking nothing! Do you hear me? Nothing!"

"Ok, ok, I hear you. I'm the same." He tensed his legs against the continuous shaking, rubbing his upper arms in an effort to heat himself up. No joy – no heat and no memory. He rubbed his head. "What the...?" His was shaved, too – prickly against his palms. Was that how he always had it? The back of his head was different, though, the skin stiff. Scabbed?

"I see they shaved your head, too," the girl said, watching him.

"Who did?"

"Oh, I dunno, let me see... How about the people who locked us to these trees?"

"Yeah, ok." He ran his fingers over the back of his head again. "Yes, I guess you're right."

"I thought you were dead when you wouldn't wake up."

He shook his head. "No, Number Eight, I'm very much alive. I do, however, appreciate your concern. Thank you very much."

Ignoring his sarcasm, she snapped to life, her blue eyes glaring at him. "Why'd you call me that?"

"Well, since you can't remember your name, I figured I'd address you by your tattoo."

She dragged herself to her feet and stared at him, her brows furrowed, then embarked on a rapid search of her body, "What? What tattoo?" Even through the dirt, it was clear to see that her arms and legs were free of any ink.

"Here." He swivelled and revealed the back of his head to her. When he turned back, she was running both hands over her scalp, her eyes widening as realisation dawned.

"What number am I?" he asked.

"What the fuck! I mean, why would anyone do that?"

All he could do was shrug. "Hey, please... My number?"

"Seven. You're Number Seven."

He didn't reply. Someone did this to them – placed them here, naked, chained, and tattooed. He checked his bound ankle. Unless they figured out a way of unlocking the bonds, they'd freeze to death before night came. They agreed they must at least work together to release themselves. But their options were slim, with nothing around heavy enough to break the lock. Any physical attempt would be in vain, as was obvious from the girl's wasted efforts.

"There must be a way out. A key or something?" He looked around. "It's either, get out of here or wait for someone to come along." An exchanged glance confirmed they didn't want to wait around for that.

Each moved about within their range in the cold dirt, searching around their respective tree, stopping every few minutes to rub arms and legs to fend off the chill.

"It's fucking useless," she shouted, giving up and sitting with her back against the tree. "There's nothing here." She sobbed into the nook of her arm.

The man kept looking. If he didn't, he feared his growing desperation would overwhelm him. How in the hell were they to get out of this? The girl wasn't much help, looking even more physically and mentally drained than him. He continued with his deliberations, but caught movement in the corner of his eye and looked to see her getting to her feet. Was she going to start searching again?

"Hey!" she shouted, nearly dancing on the spot as she looked over to his tree, "Up there. Look!"

"Huh?" He looked up, catching the smell of something foul on the slight breeze.

"There!" She jabbed a finger. "I think it's a key."

"What? Where...?"

"Right there," She jabbed again, "I think... Yes, it's tied to that branch."

Then he saw it. His stomach lurched as his gaze locked on the silvery key, tied to a branch with a black string. He looked at the girl, her eyes gleaming with excitement, then back at the key. *How the fuck am I supposed to get up there?*

"Climb up and get it," she said, as if reading his thoughts.

"Are you for real?" He held out his hands. "Look at me, I'm doing well to be able to stand."

"Don't be stupid, Mister Seven, there's no other option. We'll fucking freeze to death if we don't get out of here."

She was right, of course. Someone had carved the number seven into his head and left him here to die. He sat back on the dirt to regain some much-needed strength. Number Eight encouraged him over the next while, and they discussed how to actually get up the tree. Well, there wasn't much to discuss, with his only option being to physically climb the thing.

His first attempt ended in failure and he fell back to the ground in frustration. Number Eight rallied him on. He had to establish a technique to get his weak body up the damn thing. On the second attempt, he did better, but the bark bit into his skin, chaffing his arms and legs, forcing him to abandon and regroup. His third attempt went better – he managed to figure out a method by wrapping his arms and legs right round the trunk. Inch by inch he thrust his way upward, with every point of contact aching from the sharp bark digging into his flesh.

Number Eight shouted encouragement from below.

The chain hung like a dead weight from his ankle, but he had no choice except to keep going. With every painful shift up, he closed the distance to the first branch, giving the chain a flick to gain slack as he progressed. He almost punched the air when he reached it, but thought better. No way would he be able to do all this again if he fell. The climb had exhausted him. He grabbed hold of the branch with one hand and took a long moment to catch his breath, shaking stinging sweat from his eyes.

"Come on, you're nearly there."

"Hey, I'm up here, aren't I? Just…give me a minute."

He took a few deep breaths and got his second hand onto the branch, then pulled himself up with all his might. Number Eight whooped and clapped, but he thought better of joining in. Still a bit to go, and the effort had drained him again. He needed water, and food. The girl signalled a thumbs-up – a job well done, so far. Panting, and a little lightheaded, he returned the gesture and prepared to move again, his arms quivering as he lay outstretched along the tree's limb. The branch bent when he moved but it held his weight. It didn't help that the chain dragged at him from below. He inched forward, but the branch bowed some more and he wrapped his arms and legs tighter – the fear of falling holding him in place. So close. The key was just out of reach. If only…

"Pull the chain up," the girl shouted.

He did as she advised, swinging it closer with his leg until he caught hold of it. The clunky chunk of steel caught in the bark every step of the way. However, his efforts paid off when he hauled up enough to take most of the slack off. He balanced himself, like a snake, and snatched at the key, this time managing to knock it loose. The valuable piece of silver plummeted to the forest floor.

This time he joined in with the celebratory whoops from below, even punching the air, but it was short-lived – something rattled behind him, and it was too late by the time he realised he'd let go of the chain. The weight of it dragged him from the branch, and he barely had time to cry out before crashing to the frozen ground below.

The impact knocked the wind from his lungs, and he didn't have time to register the pain as he gagged for breath, coughing and retching, his parched tongue out in his desperation to take some air in.

"Are you all right, Mister?" the girl shouted through his fog. "Number Seven!"

Her voice pulled him out of his panic and anchored him to the moment, the transition settling enough to enable him to draw in life-enhancing breaths.

"Seven?"

"Yeah…ok," he choked out. "I… I'm…" He took a few moments to gather himself and shake off the dizziness. "I'm ok." But even with his lungs back in working order, his body burned from exhaustion – the impact had knocked every ounce of energy out of him.

"Control your breathing. Count to ten."

He shook his head, almost smiling. *If I count to one hundred, I'll still be fucked.* When he'd caught his breath and checked that his limbs were in relatively good working order, he tried the key in the lock. It went in but wouldn't turn. "Fuck! It's the wrong key."

"What? But…" She frowned, her gaze darting from left to right, obviously working it through her head. "Give it here. Let me try it in mine."

He looked at the key, then at her, then back at the key. No, there had to be a way. He tried the lock again, even angling the key, but it didn't work. Fuck!

"Come on, Seven, throw it to me."

He rubbed at the pain in his back. "And what if it works for you? How do I know you'll stay?"

"Are you serious, Mister? What am I gonna do, run through the fucking forest on my own?"

"Hey, I didn't—"

"Give me the key and I can help find yours."

He sighed and tossed the key over. The sound of her manacle unlocking was unmistakable and ground into his head. *What if she takes off? What the hell am I going to do here on my own?*

The girl removed the manacle and scrambled up with a yelp of joy, wiggling her foot with a childish delight, as if she'd never moved it before.

Then she stopped, like she realised she shouldn't be celebrating in front of him. She was right – he was happy for her, but where did it leave him? Why should she be free and not him? And why had his key released her lock and not his? She walked over to him and looked around, scanning the ground and the branches. He'd already done so, and knew that without another key, it was useless – he wasn't going anywhere.

"Please don't leave me," he said, averting his gaze from her nakedness. "There has to be another key around here somewhere. That one was clearly a test for us – some sort of task to complete."

She looked around. "Maybe I should go get help?"

"Don't be...naive. Whoever went to this much effort isn't going to let us get up and walk out of here that easily. Take a look around, there has to be another key."

She shrugged and scrambled around the nearby trees. All that surrounded them seemed to be untouched nature, with nothing out of place. He caught her glancing his way, her bottom lip turning white between her teeth. It didn't look good. What was she thinking? Was she going to head off to look for help? Or maybe just run, and keep running until she found someone. What about him? Then she shook her head, as if forcing something out of it, and turned back to him.

"Listen, Seven, if you were supposed to get my key, then it seems logical that I'm supposed to find yours."

His silent relief that she'd stayed was palpable. Best not to show it. Vulnerable enough being naked in front of each other. Naked and filthy, and starving. Damn, what he wouldn't do to eat right now.

"Are you listening to me?" she snapped.

"Yes, of course. All we can do is search. You continue with the outer reaches and I'll work around my tree."

"But we've already searched. I mean, where else can it be?"

He was just about to answer along the lines of not knowing, when he noticed a patch of dirt near her tree – a different colour to the surface around it. "Over there, look." He pointed. "There's a bit of a mound there, different to the rest."

She looked along his arm and finger and ran over. Using her fingers, she clawed away at the clay and dug into the earth, then squealed with delight when she retrieved a silver key.

"Yes!" he roared, tears of relief brimming in his eyes. "Quick, Eight, quick, bring it over."

She sprinted over and unlocked the manacle around his ankle. He groaned when it fell off, grimacing at the sting from the flayed flesh where the steel had cut in.

However, he didn't care. They were free from their shackles, and that's what counted. Time to get out of this nightmare.

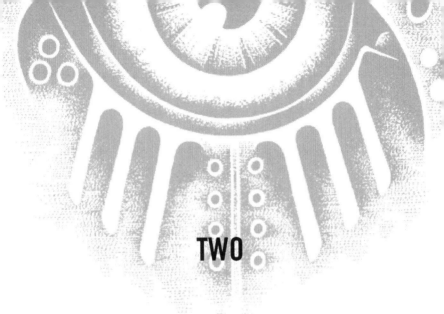

TWO

The naked pair wandered through the woods, making their way between trees in what they hoped was a straight course towards escape or help. With the forest being mostly dark and silent, they had no real way of knowing which way was which. The bark on the trees had no moss or lichen, and the canopy caused shadows to gather in all directions across the forest floor.

The man – Seven – searched the corners of his mind to remember something, anything, before his awakening, but nothing of substance came to him other than disconnected flashes: a vision of a man – possibly himself – with long brown hair tied into a bun, cycling through busy streets. *London?* He stopped in his tracks. *Am I a Londoner?* No, can't be. Not with an accent that screamed Irish.

There was no telling if these fragments were real or figments of delusion. Then images of an office flitted across his mind, where he sat at a desk, casually dressed, with code scrolling across his PC's screen at a rapid rate. Perhaps some sort of IT gig? He couldn't be sure. But the one thing he was clear about was the image of the woman he loved. A shiver raced across his shoulders. His wife? Girlfriend? The relationship status didn't matter at this point. She was there and that was the only certainty he had, albeit nothing but a small, vivid silhouette. He loved her, unlike his job, whatever it was. For all he knew, he may have been the UK's Prime Minister – a thought that made him smile.

The girl seemed to be deep in thought, too, probably catching glimpses of a young woman doing something somewhere she couldn't quite grasp. Like him, she wasn't sure who she was, or how she'd got here. She'd told him she could picture a college and possibly a graduation, but nothing beyond that. And certainly nothing before waking in the woods. She rubbed the scabs on the back of her scalp and shook her head.

Though he didn't say it, not wanting to scare her any further, he knew in his gut that what was happening was no accident. As they wandered along, trying to figure out which direction they were heading in, a sickening smell grabbed their attention. Instead of moving away from it, they decided to follow it. If anything, it might lead them to some form of civilisation – some answer. With every cautious step, moving from the cover of each tree, it grew stronger, until they came to its source – a grey chain-link fence, about ten-foot high, with razor wire looping along its top. Fused to it were bodies – dozens of them – all naked, their charred remains blackened and reeking from the stench of electrified death and decomposition.

Eight gasped in horror at the sight, turning into Seven's chest to shield her vision from the hordes of flies, swarming and crawling all over the poor souls.

Seven held her tight, unable to look away from the burnt remains of these people who so obviously had tried to escape from their harrowing predicament, or simply chose an easy out. Whatever the reason, Seven and Eight embraced as the realisation of their reality dawned. Beyond the fence stood nothing but trees as far as the eye could see, and they were obviously on the wrong side of it. He scanned along the structure until it was swallowed up in the far distance by the forest. *We're trapped.*

The eerie silence broke with the sound of a woman's scream, from the direction they'd just come from, or so he guessed, considering the echoing effect of so many trees around them. He grabbed the young girl and ducked back into the woods and beneath an earth bank. "Hang on," he whispered, "let's wait here a second."

"It sounds like someone's in trouble?" she said.

"We're the ones who're in trouble here," he snapped.

The scream roared up through the trees again. Then, "Help! Help me, please!"

The girl pulled at his arm. "We have to go help her."

He ripped free of her grasp and turned her to him, hands on shoulders. "Are you mad? We could be walking into a trap."

"But she needs help."

Before he could respond, she shrugged free of him and took off towards the continuous cries.

Icy shivers gripped him as his heartbeat pounded through his ears, his sweat stinging his eyes. *Fuck! What the hell am I doing here?* Nothing felt right. It was all too surreal to comprehend. But at the same time, he couldn't stay where he was. He ran after the girl.

They passed numerous trees, the screams echoing in the brisk air, until they arrived at a ridge – a gap in the ground, possibly forged many years before by a river or flood. A woman lay at the bottom of the embankment. Like they had been, she was naked and chained to a tree, except she hung upside down from her manacled ankle. Her shaved scalp also bore a fresh tattoo – the number Two. Number Two was older than him, probably old enough to be his mother.

That threw him, because he couldn't bring up a visual of his mother. He pushed the effort aside and focused on the problem at hand. This poor woman was frail, shaking from the cold, with blood oozing from beneath the steel clamped around her ankle. She'd obviously exhausted herself struggling against her predicament and made the wound worse by doing so.

Despite her distressed state, she had the strength to fill the space with another scream.

"Hey! Hey now, we're here." Eight crawled down the bank to distressed woman.

Seven watched from above, glancing around to make sure they weren't under threat. However they'd got into this situation, it didn't take a degree in rocket science to figure out that they were in deep shit, probably the deepest he'd ever been in – if he could remember what had come before.

The old woman's tree stood on the opposite bank, and he reckoned she'd been in her upside-down position for quite some time, what with her ankle injury and her utter exhaustion. He looked around once more, then climbed down to join Eight.

"There must be a key – like there was with our chains," Eight said, scanning their immediate area. She grimaced and shrugged. "Her ankle is in bad shape."

They tried to comfort Two, but she wouldn't respond, just continuing to shriek and cry, snot bubbling from her nose. Each scream shot a wave of panic through Seven, his heart pounding as the forest swirled and closed in on him.

"Hey!" Eight shouted at him. "You're drifting. Stay with me here."

While he heard her, it was as if she stood beyond – outside – her words not connecting. The forest swirled again and black spots clouded the edges of his vision. He reached up to steady himself and stop the trees from spinning, but they moved too fast.

Something clicked in the distance, over and over. Was it his past trying to reconnect? Eight was waving, miles away. Why was she so far away from him? He needed her here, to stop the trees.

Then his head smashed into the heavens and he hit the ground. Everything became still. *Fuck!* He looked up at Eight standing over him, rubbing her hand. His cheek stung and he held his cold palm against its heat.

"Don't have me do that again," she said. "Go see if you can get her foot free."

He shook his head clear and followed the chain up the bank to the tree, dragging himself the final few feet. *Got to focus.* He needed food and water if he was to keep going. *C'mon, man. Concentrate.*

Just like his restraint, the chain was padlocked around the pine. He looked for possible burial sites for a key, but nothing unnatural or different stood out to him. Maybe in the branches?

The prospect of another agonising climb didn't sit well with him, but he'd do it if he had to. He looked up but, again, nothing. "There's no key. No-one else chained up, or anything around here. Only trees and dirt."

Eight looked up at him. "Okay. We have to do something. If we don't get this chain off her leg soon, she could bleed out, or die of shock."

Seven climbed back down and studied Two's ankle. The cuts were deep, her blood pouring from around the manacle, the flesh open to the bone in places. He held her foot and ran his fingers around the steel. "I could probably manoeuvre it through."

Eight looked at him with wide eyes as she rested Two's head on her lap, "You're serious?"

He shrugged, then whispered to the woman, "Madam, I can try to get you free this way. Can I try?" He watched for a response, but the woman was lost in a state of delirium, struggling and jostling within Eight's arms.

"Just go for it," Eight snapped. "Fuck it, we have no alternative."

Seven gripped the ankle and chain, then put pressure on the dug-in manacle. As it shifted, it took her bloodied flesh with it, but he had no choice if he was to create leverage to bring it over her heel. Blood soaked his hands and hindered his grip.

The woman howled again, so much louder than before. Panic welling in him as he struggled to keep a grasp on the situation.

"Damn it," Eight cried, "take a deep breath and force it!"

Using Two's blood to lubricate her ankle, and bending her foot, he applied more pressure to the shackle. It worked to an extent, but not enough. He looked around in a desperate attempt to find something to help. With nothing but dry cold dirt surrounding them, and the woman's howls filling his head, he had no choice but to keep going. He took a deep breath and pulled with all his might.

The manacle slipped free with a loud snap and Eight had to grab hold of the old woman to prevent her slipping down the slope. Two's horrific screams reverberated through their immediate area.

"Did you just break her ankle?" Eight asked, fear and dread filling her eyes.

He looked at her, his mouth open. They had to get her free. What else could he do? "I'm sorry. I'm so sorry." He dropped the bloodied chain, leaving it dangling from the tree, and went to see if he could help.

Eight retched and gagged, but nothing more than a string of bile came out.

The elderly woman grabbed the back of his neck and whispered something into his ear, but before he could decipher her words, her eyes rolled up and she collapsed back into Eight's arms, unconscious.

THREE

Seven and Eight struggled to carry Two along with them – the injury to her leg packed with handfuls of mulch. It was the best they could do and it would have to suffice for now, but they needed to find something to help clean the wound. They each had an arm draped across their shoulders, continuing to move in what felt like a downhill direction, mainly in the hope that it might lead them to water. Several times they stopped and listened, hoping for the sound that would save their lives; the gentle flow of a forest stream.

Seven couldn't get over how fast the light was fading. One minute it filtered through gaps in the canopy, next it was like they were surrounded by a heavy dusk, and with it a creeping night chill that brought goosebumps to every part of him. Their already depleted energy levels had them gasping for breath, stopping at increasingly regular intervals to regain enough strength to carry on. The freezing air stung the tips of his ears, and his joints throbbed with the impact of every step.

He had no idea when he'd last eaten – it might have been days, and probably more considering the constant grumbling and groaning from his stomach. But that was nothing to the sharp, acidic pain creeping through him, as if something had drilled its way in through the back of his head and into his mind. Probably just a headache brought on from dehydration.

Darkness engulfed the forest.

"What the...?" He looked around, shocked at the sudden onset of what seemed to be deep night. "That was fast. We'll have to stop, I can barely see a thing."

"She needs a hospital," Eight said, helping him lay Two on the ground.

"We all need a fucking hospital," he snapped.

"Yes, but you're not the one bleeding to death. That lump of muck isn't stopping the flow."

He looked at Two's wound, covered with dirt they'd scraped from the forest floor in an effort to staunch the blood. She was right, it wasn't working. "Okay, but burning ourselves out walking in the dark isn't going to get us there any sooner. Wherever *there* is."

Her shoulders dropped in quiet acquiescence. He saw it in her eyes. Like him, she was too tired and scared to fight.

Consumed by exhaustion, with both struggling to breathe easy, they rested themselves as best they could. Seven's heartbeat drummed through his ears, with each breath deepening the chill within. As the night went on, the absolute silence and pitch darkness weighed on him like a solid block.

Then it came to him. At first, he couldn't believe what he was hearing, questioned it when for so long before he'd heard nothing. The prospect of salvation sparked him to life and he was on his feet before he knew it. "Can you hear that?"

Neither woman responded.

He stepped towards the sound, unable to see a thing, but certain his ears weren't lying to him. Or were they? *Maybe I'm just hearing what I want to hear?* That stopped him in his tracks.

"Hey? Hey, girl? Eight? Can you hear me?"

Nothing. *What the hell is going on?* He felt around on the ground for them – he'd been close earlier – but could only find frozen dirt, crisp with frost. No way could he go out there on his own, and he daren't move further for fear of creating distance between himself and the women. He had no choice but to hunker down, hug his knees tight, and try to conserve his body heat until the light returned.

~

Time passed, and he eventually managed to doze, constantly chased by abstract and disconnected visuals he couldn't stop long enough to gain any sense of. When he opened his eyes next, morning was breaking, with a dim light filtering through the canopy and onto the forest floor. All around him tall trees stretched to the skyline. It hadn't been a dream – he was here, trapped, and starving. Then he remembered what he'd heard and he struggled to his feet, his limbs stiff and his muscles screaming their pain straight to his head.

A short distance away, the two women lay cuddled together beneath a film of frost. Panic shot through him as he ran over, quivering. "No, please, no. I can't be alone in this place."

He leaned over and reached out, his hand shaking. While they were cold, their flesh was soft – subtle to the touch, and when he noticed a gentle plume of vapour appearing beneath Eight's nostrils, a stifling relief coursed through him, bringing tears to his eyes.

Taking pains not to frighten her, he shook the girl's shoulder, then stepped back when her eyes flickered open and she looked up at him.

"I...think there's water – a river – over there somewhere. Listen, can you hear it?"

Eight extricated herself from Two and groaned as she got to her feet. She had to cough and slap her chest several times before she could reply. Then she closed her eyes and listened, for what seemed an age.

When she opened her eyes, she simply nodded. "Okay, let's go. I don't know how much more I can take."

"What about her?"

"All we can do is pack her wound and take her with us. It doesn't sound like it's too far."

They did this, but he knew that without medical attention it was likely to become infected, if it wasn't already. When they picked her up, she groaned, but with their combined effort, they managed to hoist her enough to carry her forward.

Two seemed to gain weight with every laboured footstep, but working as a team, they developed a rhythm and pace that saw them only stopping every so often – long enough to catch their breaths and solidify their hold on their patient. Even with the struggle, Seven kept part of his focus on point, until he heard that beautiful sound above everything else and knew he hadn't been hallucinating.

"It's close." His tongue felt bigger and courser now the reality was upon them. Then he smelled it – like clear, pristine air, drawing him forward without any effort or waste of energy. When they reached the bank, they lay Two on the ground and crawled down to the running water, unable to resist the compulsion to fill their depleted bodies with this pure elixir of life.

For the first time since they met, they shared a smile. Seven drank and drank, until he couldn't take in another drop. Life sparked its way through him, from his stomach into his limbs, his chest, his head – everywhere.

Eight cupped handful after handful, first splashing it against her face, then massaged herself with it, whimpering with delight. It changed everything. She turned her attention to their patient, carrying handfuls of water up the bank and trying to get her to drink, but most of it ended up running off the side of her face. Instead, she opted to clean the old woman's wound.

Seven scanned downriver along the bank. He wasn't certain if that was downhill, with the landscape looking so level on all sides, but it had to be. Everything surrounding them bore the signs of winter. Nothing but trees, dense in most places, with the forest floor covered in a mix of dry dirt, frost patches, and the odd stone – all of this surrounded by a fence that could kill at the faintest touch. His thoughts drifted, but not enough to miss something he swore was real. A tree, off in the distance, shimmered, almost hologram like – probably the last of the dehydration playing tricks. Now, though, it looked just like the others. He lifted his gaze skywards, but the few gaps in the canopy showed nothing but erratic cloud movement.

A crazy place, with nothing but barren wilderness beneath the mass of trees.

They sat in silence beside Two, watching the stream's slow but constant progress. Though nothing had been said, Seven knew what Eight was thinking – it was just a matter of who would say it first. The old woman was a hindrance. No way could they continue under her burden, even with water close at hand. She couldn't be left behind, but was there enough trust to remain in the hope the other would return with help?

His thoughts were interrupted by the sound of snapping twigs that shot a burst of butterflies through his gut and chest. Eight stared at him, her eyes wide in fear. They got to their feet and stood beside each other, facing the sounds coming at a fast pace from the densest part of the forest on the other side of the stream. He stepped in front of her, not sure what was coming, but ready to face whatever the woods were about to reveal. Was it a bear? A pack of wolves? Eight grasped his arms and they braced for the impending onslaught.

The noise grew louder and closer, now with muffled cries echoing through the trees.

He looked at Eight. "People?"

She grimaced as she shrugged.

"It might be help," he said.

She didn't respond, instead running the few steps to the bank where she picked up a stone she could barely carry with both hands.

Seven stared at her, arms out in silent query. A stone she couldn't handle wouldn't be much help, especially if they were outnumbered. Then the noise stopped and they held their breaths in anticipation, searching the shadows beyond the treeline above the opposite bank.

"Hey! I found them," a woman called. "Down by the river! Here!"

The woman, dressed in grey rags, stepped out and stood staring at them. A moment later, two men joined her, all three with bristled heads. They walked down to the bank, and Seven noticed as they looked around that each had a numbered tattooed on the back of their skull. He shivered at the prospect of being dressed, even if it was in grey rags. One of the men was young, about the same age as Eight. The woman was older, with a stern look on her face, and the other man had brown skin and a physique that had once been developed but was now faded.

The woman signalled to the younger man. "Go back and tell Charlie we found them."

The lad didn't hesitate, stepping back into the shadows, the forest floor creaking beneath his quick feet.

"Who are you people?" Eight called, her voice edged with fear. "Where are we? What the hell is going on here?"

The woman smiled, her dark eyes lighting up. "We'll tell you all when we get back to the camp. You guys need some food in your bellies, and that woman clearly needs help."

Seven and Eight didn't put up a fight. What choice did they have? Both of them had no memory of how they'd arrived here. They were cold and naked, and the prospect of food was more than enough to see them moving without protest. Camps in the woods generally had fires, hot food and drink. Or so they hoped...

The brown-skinned man and Seven hoisted Two up and made their way off in the direction from which the strangers had come – leaving the woman to bring Eight along. As twigs bent and snapped underfoot, Seven glanced at Eight and hoped they weren't walking into a trap.

FOUR

Richard...? Is that you, mate?" someone with a husky voice called over as Seven entered the campsite. At first, it didn't register that he was being addressed by a real name. The person repeated it three more times, and with that it was as if part of his memory block unlocked. From within the darkness, an image emerged. *I am Richard* – or Richie, as his friends back home knew him. *Hold on, someone here knows me?* He looked at the wretched group of men and women huddled around a small fire in the middle of the camp, but couldn't figure out who'd called out to him. Including himself and his two companions, there were nine in total at the camp, with nine makeshift beds forming an extended circle around the flames.

"Welcome," an elderly man said from within the group. He stood at an impressive height that singled him out from the rest. His head was stubbled with white spikes, a faint echo of a crown that once sported grey hair. The number one tattooed on the back of his head was scabbed and blistered – not a great job compared to some of the others. Despite his height, he was overweight, yet frail – skin hung from his limbs and, like the others, he was wrapped in rags. His face bore a striking resemblance to Boris Johnson, which amused Richard as he and Eight were invited to join the group around the fire.

"Stacy, please help Carol look after that woman," the old man ordered in a crackly voice, his words clipped and clear. A young woman sprang up and rushed to attend to the unconscious Two.

As Richard looked around, he realised that, apart from the beds and fire, the camp was bare of any equipment. Everyone else looked hungry, tired, and cold, and all of them had their heads shaved and freshly tattooed.

"Ok, what the hell is going on here?" he demanded. "Where are we? And why are we here?"

"Patience, my dear man," the old guy said in his posh English accent, his open hand up in a placating gesture. "My name is Charles. Welcome to the camp. We knew there were more of you out there, and thankfully we have won this task by locating you and bringing you here."

Richard turned to Eight, who frowned and shook her head, "What task?" he muttered.

"Never mind that now," Charles said. "Come sit by the fire. Ian will get you something to wear, and we have warm soup for you. Unfortunately, it has no meat in it – only a basic vegetable soup. However, it will warm your insides."

Someone handed them their ration in a grubby bowl, but the rags could wait – the food took priority over anything else. With a snort, Richard slurped it down.

"Don't rush it, old chap," Charles advised. "It is likely you haven't eaten in quite a while. You don't want to cramp up."

Cramp was nothing to the pain and discomfort he'd experienced since waking in the woods, and this guy wanted them to go easy on the food? He looked around at everyone staring at them. Surreal, or what? Then the headache returned. His vision blurred while he weathered the storm. When it cleared, he edged closer to the fire to feel its heat.

Carol and Stacy made the old woman comfortable near the flames. Even so, she was in a dire state, slumped and motionless on her camp bed.

"How'd you know my name?" Richard asked, looking from one to the other to see who would answer. When he locked eyes on a man standing to his left, something inside shifted – another patch of blocked memory edging free.

"Richie, it's me?" The man walked towards him. "Don't you remember, mate? It's me, Tom."

Tom? Tom...? Yes, Tom, from back home. A friend? Was he? "Yes, sorry, Tom. Of course!" He shook his head. "Forgive me, I'm having trouble remembering stuff. Well, anything, really." He glanced around the gathering. "I woke up yesterday deep in the woods and I... I don't know."

"Let me guess, foggy memory?" Charles waved his hand across his brow. "Headaches drilling into the back of your head? You are not alone with that. The rest of us also woke up in this wider area." A couple of them nodded in agreement. "This is no accident, Richard. Indeed, somebody made this camp and fenced us all in here."

"Who did?" Eight snapped, startling almost everyone. "What's going on here?"

Charles held his open hand up again. "I shall tell you what I know. But first, you two need to relax, drink your soup, and try to let your minds settle."

Any semblance of sun was blocked out by the thick canopy above the campsite, and eight of the nine huddled around the fire to keep warm and to allow Richard and Eight to finish their first meal in days.

After a good while, Charles got to his feet. "Right, chaps, let us get the formalities out of the way, shall we? We are all here now, aren't we? First, let's hear from our new arrivals. As I said, chaps, my name is Charles." He extended his hand to Richard.

"Richard, apparently," he answered with a nervous snigger, then looked to Eight and shrugged.

She took a long breath, "Tiffany. Or Tiff."

He glared at her. "I thought you couldn't remember anything?"

"A few things came back to me this morning. I just didn't want to get into it." Her soft voice hinted at a youthful innocence, some distance from the sharp tone before.

"I am sure we all have a lot of questions for one another," Charles said, "but first, let's get the obvious out of the way. We all have a new feature on our scalps, don't we? So, I shall go in numerical order." He stepped away from the group and turned to show his tattoo. "From what I am told, I have the number one." He turned back. "My name is Charles. I can't recall my surname, but from what I remember, I believe, outside of this place, I was enjoying some sort of retirement."

He pointed over to the unconscious woman, still slumped on her camp bed. "This old dear has the number two. Did anyone happen to catch her name?"

Everyone shook their heads.

"That is a pity. But for now, we will continue on in order. Shall we?"

The brown-skinned man, built like a boxer, stood and revealed the number three on his head. "My name is Nabil," he announced, his accent a mix of Mancunian and Middle Eastern. "I woke up here yesterday chained to a tree, but my memory is faded, and I dunno how I got here."

He looked familiar to Richard, but he couldn't place him.

Nobody asked any questions. The next to stand was the stern-faced woman in or about her thirties. Her look said *approach with care,* the kind of person who should carry a warning sign around their neck. She had *four* on the back of her head, with dried blood still visible beneath the tattoo where it had dribbled down her neck. "I'm Stacy. That's all I've got. Can't remember anything before Charles picked me up out there in the woods."

After a few moments of silence, the young lad stood. He'd been branded with the number five. His eyes were filled with hurt and pain, his body thin and gaunt, with his skin taut across his cheekbones and brow, giving his face a skeletal look. "My name is... Ian," he stammered, his voice shaking. "Nnn...nice to meet you." Then he sank into himself and began to sob. "I want to go home."

Next was Number Six. A woman in her fifties stood with real confidence. She gave Ian a hug. "There, there. Sit down, my dear."

She watched as the broken lad returned to his position at the fire. "He's having an emotional time trying to cope with all of this. My name is Carol. I suppose I am the mammy of the group." Her mammy joke was met with silence. "Back in the real world, I am a nurse in the London Bridge Hospital. Can't remember much outside of that. But before I woke up in this place, I was working a night shift. Things get a little hazy after that and, I suppose, here I am."

Everyone turned and looked at Seven.

Richard didn't stand. Instead, he took a sip of hot water from a clay cup beside the pot warming by the fire. "As you all probably heard, I'm Richard. Or Richie, as I think my friends call me. Woke up chained to a tree near Tiffany. I think I was working in London prior to that, but can't be sure."

This was met with a collective head nod.

Eight looked around and shrugged. "Hi, Guys. My name is Tiffany and I am from Essex. Everyone calls me, Tiff. And I—"

"This isn't a fucking job interview," Tom barked, his voice as harsh as his words. His eyes boiled with anger as he stood and towered over the group. "I'm number nine because some cunt shaved my head and branded me. And when I find the prick, I am going to carve him up really good."

Charles stood and patted Tom's shoulder – probably the only one who could have done such a thing at that moment without becoming the recipient of the angry man's wrath. "Sit down,

Tom. That's quite enough for now. We are all overwhelmed and scared here."

"So, what's the plan now, old man? Tell fucking campfire stories and sing Kumbaya? Hold on while I break out the marshmallows."

"No," Charles answered, keeping his tone gentle. "As we determined earlier, there are nine sets of bedding in camp, which means all nine of us are here now. And please don't be under any illusions – we were all put in this compound for a reason."

Tom looked to the canopy and growled. "I know that, Chucky. But this is against my will." He looked around the camp. "I want fucking answers and I want to get the fuck out of here."

Richard remembered Tom from work, but it was a bit vague. *Was he a friend, or just a colleague?* He'd always been an angry cockney – that was for sure. Good company for after-work drinks, which was great after having moved to London from Ireland and only getting to know people. Tom helped him plug into the local social scene. A cold wave shot through him. *My wife?* Visuals flooded back. He had a beautiful wife. Elizabeth – or Lizzy, as her friends and family knew her. *Or did she hate that name?* Confusion washed over him again. *Why is this happening to me? Why can't I remember crap before waking up in this place?* He winced from the pain pounding into his brain, like a spike buried inside his skull.

"Ok, Tom," Charles said, "we need to be calm. Let's discuss what we do know, shall we?"

"Hey, you're the self-appointed chief. Knock yourself out, Boss."

Charles took a moment to clear his throat. "Okay, where was that poor dear found?" He nodded towards Two.

"Richie and I found her chained to a tree," Tiffany answered. "She had fallen into a ditch and hung upside down until we came along."

"Okay, well, there you have it, chaps. All nine of us woke up in this forest, disorientated and shackled to one of these fine pine trees. All of our memories are hazy and, yet, each of us managed to find our way to this campsite, where, magically, there is bedding for all, water, some cutlery, and the means to make some soup and start a fire. This is no coincidence, let me tell you."

The group uttered a collective groan as they nodded agreement.

"Why us?" Richard asked. "Why us nine?"

"Never mind the why, Richie, mate," Tom said, "you should be asking, who is watching, and why?"

Richard looked to where Tom pointed. "These little buggers are all around us and watching our every move."

He scanned each tree and branch, struggling to accept that there were dozens of tiny cameras hanging well out of reach. Like little black bubbles, their spidery eyes glinting.

"We're being watched," Tom announced, "and whoever is on the other side of the lens did this. Stripped us naked, chained us up, and put us on the wrong side of that electric fence."

"Did you see the dead bodies, too?" Tiff asked. Tom didn't answer but Charles nodded in the affirmative.

"I'm getting my strength back," Nabil said, breaking the silence. "And once I'm ready, I'm following that river downstream and getting the fuck out of here. This is nothing more than a sick joke and I'm not laughing."

The group didn't argue with his sentiment, with many obviously having come through a similar experience to Richard and Tiffany, still shattered and bruised from their ordeal. The water and food provided would have to do for now, and getting some rest was all most could think about. Two, silent and still on the camp bed, needed urgent medical attention, but no one could even begin to think about playing doctor to her. It was all too much. They talked among themselves, trying to piece together the fragments of memory in an effort to find out who they were. Nothing concrete could be laid, but some minor personality traits were recalled. Carol mentioned a fear of heights, while Charles remembered a fear of death

– which amused Richard, as the old man didn't look too far away from facing that.

Amongst the chatter about fear, death, and wishes, Richard couldn't help but notice how organised Stacey was. Her bed was as clean as it could be under the circumstances, and she was constantly cleaning beneath her nails with twigs. Mild OCD, or some sort of mysophobia? That was one trait he could recall about his wife, but then the headache came back.

He rested as best he could for the rest of the evening. At one stage, he looked up and thought he glimpsed the moon glowing through the canopy, but he couldn't be sure. He couldn't be sure of anything, except for the deafening silence that accompanied the bone-numbing chill around the camp. As far as he could tell, everyone was awake, just lying on their beds wrapped in rags and trying to keep warm. The forest cloaked them, but also held them prisoner, its looming silence occasionally broken by one of the group shifting beneath their blanket, or by a camera buzzing as its lens adjusted.

Thoughts of home filled his head, and what he could puzzle together from disjointed memories. The day he and Lizzy moved in together floated past like an old movie replaying in his mind's eye. She announced her pregnancy and gave him the ultimatum: get a real job or... From beyond the headache, his role in fatherhood came to him. His heartbeat skipped at the thought of being a father, but the child's face, or anything about it, wouldn't come to him. He shifted it to the side and focused back on her offer – well, ultimatum. Things would have to change. His job wouldn't cover rent, never mind a mortgage. How long ago had that been? Was his son or daughter waiting for him at home? Where was home? He couldn't remember his occupation – but was ninety-nine percent certain it involved computers. At the very least, he sat in front of one all day. He needed to get home. Nabil was right. At first light, they had to get out of this place.

FIVE

The silence was shattered by a loud static crackling throughout the camp, almost like a klaxon, causing everyone to jump. Richard shot up and looked around in the darkness, honing in on the sound of a radio struggling to find a tuning. It seemed to come from near the campfire, its embers now giving little light.

Several called out in confusion. Charles barked orders to get the fire going, and Tom and Nabil scrambled to place wood on it. "He's coming back, chaps."

"Who is?" Tiffany cried. "Who's coming back?"

"The one who tasked us to bring you three back to camp," Charles replied. "Now hurry up and line up."

It took a while, but flames eventually flickered, lighting everyone's faces as they all looked at the same thing – a silver pole standing a few feet from the fire. The smooth cylinder was about three feet in height, with a battered black-mesh speaker cover on top, from which static continued to crackle and hum.

"What the fuck is that thing?" Richard asked, stepping over to inspect the foreign object. "Was this always here?"

"No need to panic," Charles said, "just listen."

Richard looked around the base of the pole, where the dirt had been disturbed. "Looks like it came out of the ground." Nobody seemed to hear him.

Tiff ran her hands over the cylinder. "How do you make it stop? Is there a button or switch on it? Someone make it stop, please."

Then, as if reacting to Tiff's touch, the static was replaced by a faint voice, the audio low and difficult to make out.

"What's it saying this time?" Carol asked.

Nobody answered.

The hairs across Richard's shoulders bristled when the volume slowly rose to reveal a voice counting down from sixty. A man's voice – deep, robotic, with an almost Russian-sounding inflection.

Tiffany and Stacy huddled together, but Carol stood alone, like the men, all staring in anticipation of what would happen when the countdown reached zero. When it did, the crackling flames filled the silence.

PARTICIPANTS.

WELCOME TO BLOCK EIGHTEEN.

YOU HAVE ALL BEEN CAREFULLY SELECTED TO TAKE PART IN THIS SPECIAL EXERCISE.

I AM HOST.

INSTRUCTIONS WILL BE TRANSMITTED BY ME DURING YOUR TIME HERE.

FAILURE TO COMPLY WITH INSTRUCTIONS. PENALTY.

YOUR INITIATION OBJECTIVE: LOCATE PARTICIPANT, TWO, SEVEN, AND EIGHT...

COMPLETE.

REWARD: BASIC CLOTHING. FOOD. REST PERIODS.

UNAUTHORIZED WITHDRAWAL FROM DESIGNATED AREA WILL RESULT IN INFRACTION.

INFRACTIONS WILL NOT BE TOLERATED.

OBJECTIVES: DURING YOUR TIME IN BLOCK EIGHTEEN, YOU WILL EACH BE SELECTED TO PERFORM AN OBJECTIVE OUTLINED BY YOUR HOST.

COMPLETED OBJECTIVES WILL RESULT IN REWARD.

FAILURE TO COMPLETE OBJECTIVE WILL RESULT IN INFRACTION.

SELECTION FOR OBJECTIVE WILL BE BASED ON PARTICIPANT PROFILE.

DETAILED PROFILES HAVE NOW BEEN UPLOADED.

OBJECTIVE PROCESSING WILL BE SUBJECT TO THE FOLLOWING ATTRIBUTES:

PERSONAL HISTORY. MENTAL CAPABILITY. PHYSICAL ENDURANCE.

BLOCK EIGHTEEN IS SUBJECT TO TWENTY-FOUR-SEVEN SURVEILLANCE.

WARNING: DO NOT TOUCH EQUIPMENT.

EXERCISE TO BE MONITORED BY SUBSCRIPTION MEMBERS.

OBJECTIVE ONE WILL COMMENCE AT SIX A.M.

PARTICIPANTS MUST BE READY FOR ROLL CALL.

The silver pole lowered back into the ground and the group stared at the spot, all in shock at what they'd just witnessed and heard.

"This is bollocks," Tom snapped. "Someone is having a laugh here." He stomped his way back over to his bed. "I'm with you, Nabil. First thing in the morning, we are walking down that river and leaving this prick's mind games behind. Pure bollocks."

"Are you gonna be the first to test what an infraction is then?" Stacy asked. "And what about the objectives?"

"Like I said, love, this is all a load of bollocks. Nothing more than an elaborate prank. Oh, let's see how they all react when we put them into one of those red rooms. MTV Punk'd for normal Londoners. Come off it."

Nabil nodded in agreement, but his eyes showed fear.

The transmission from The Host sounded pre-recorded and had affected them all. Even Charles, who had been somewhat positive up to this point, now sat in silence.

Richard studied the old man's body language – slumped over his knees, defeated. Ian and the two younger women were in tears, the three of them sitting on one bed.

At Charles' suggestion, they all huddled together for warmth while they tried to sleep through the rest of the night. Most of them slipped off into a cold slumber, possibly thinking about a story Charles had told them earlier in the day, when they'd made their makeshift bedding on the ground – penguins in Antarctica, and how they kept warm during the winter months by sleeping together.

It was at this point Richard realised that this group of strangers was mentally broken. He agreed with Tom – fuck this game reserve, at first light, it was time to get away from this madness.

SIX

Lashing rain woke them as morning light slid in between the trees. No time was wasted, with the forest floor crackling under the weight of men moving at a steady pace, working their way between trees and low-lying branches.

Tom, Nabil, Richard, and Ian had set out with a mission in mind, and carried nothing but their raggy clothes.

Ian, always struggling to keep pace, brought up the rear, but still managed to keep within sight. The plan was to follow the stream's path, the theory being that it would eventually lead them to the sea, or a lake. Unlike the fence, which they concluded must have run in a large circle.

They stopped for a third time to catch their breath in what seemed to be a never-ending wilderness.

"This fucking forest is endless," Tom said, gasping for air.

No one answered. They didn't have to, because everyone knew they needed to press on. Their mission wasn't just to escape, but to send help back to the stricken Two, whose leg was worse than ever. Its colour that morning signalled that infection had set in, and if it went untreated, she would soon be consumed with septicaemia or something equally as horrific. She needed real medical attention, and they were her only hope.

As he drank from the stream, Richard couldn't help think about The Host and what had been said. Objectives based on their mental and physical endurance? And penalties and infractions – what the fuck was that about? No, everything about it felt wrong. These woods had no life other than the stream, with no plants, birds, or the smell of fresh pine anyone would expect in the forest – instead, a faint stink of something rotting hung in the air. Still, the rest did him good, and somewhere inside he was grateful for it.

Ian sat in silence, staring into the stream's gentle ripples.

Richard felt for him. The lad was skin and bone, and if they had been selected for a reason, it baffled him what someone like Ian would offer in a situation like this. That said, he didn't take no for an answer when Tom rounded them up for the escape. Perhaps beneath that weak exterior, a brave heart thundered. Or maybe he was just desperate to get home. Either way, he was here now, and like it or not he was one of the team.

"Let's keep moving," Nabil whispered. He pointed up into the trees. "I might be wrong, but these cameras don't seem to be tracking us yet."

Richard scanned the branches. "I don't know. Might be naïve to think they haven't followed our progress."

"Come on, mate," Tom said, "nothing has intercepted us yet. Don't you think they'd have nabbed us if they knew we'd scarpered?"

"And they're not moving," Nabil added.

Richard looked from one beady-eyed camera to another. Nabil was right, none of them moved or seemed to focus in or out.

"Fuck that tin can," Tom said. "Nothing more than a sick joke. Let's go. Sitting here waiting around is only playing into the cunts' hand."

All Richard could do was shrug and move on with them, Tom's words replaying in his mind. *A tin can?* No, it wasn't that simple. Block 18, as primitive as it was for the participants, was anything but for those running the show. He thought about who could have created such a place? And who could put their fellow man through such an ordeal? Whoever it was, had to be evil. Someone with no regard for humanity, who wanted to gain nothing more than to dehumanize people for pleasure. The longer this *game* went on, the weaker they'd all become. And although their health was diminishing, they had no choice but to power through.

Escape was essential, and it would have to happen now or never.

SEVEN

With no word of how the men were faring, a sense of unease had crept into the camp. Charles couldn't help but ponder on the possible scenarios if the escape party returned or not? He figured he'd give them at least a day before he'd start panicking.

Stacy and Tiffany went off to collect wood for the fire, while Carol and Charles tried their best to tend to Two's ghastly leg wound.

"The poor dear is running out of time," he said.

"Is that your idea of bedside manner, Charles?" Stress and worry were etched across her face, with deep shadows under her eyes.

"No, no, of course not. I am merely stating the obvious, my dear. I prefer to be a realist when it comes to these things." He pulled a raggy cloth over his head, but it made no difference with the rain continuing to pelt down. "Unless this Host chap has some antibiotics and sterile dressings, this poor woman is in real danger. As it stands, her leg is deeply infected."

"So, we can do nothing for her, is that what you're saying?"

"I am just giving my opinion, my dear. You're the healthcare professional. If you can think of something better for her, I'm all ears." He got up and left Carol to do her best for Two, acknowledging her frustration at being unable to help in any discernible way.

The girls returned with a few scraps of wood – Stacy appearing agitated.

"What's the matter, my dear?" he asked.

She didn't reply. Instead, Tiff explained that the lack of sanitized conditions was starting to really get to her.

They huddled around the fire, trying their hardest to keep warm. Charles endeavoured to comfort Stacy by downplaying her phobia. But it was no use – she'd retreated inside her head and refused to talk about it.

"We all fear something..." Carol said, her gaze fixed on the flames.

"Oh, yeah, yours is heights, right?" Tiff's teeth chattered from the cold.

"Yes."

Charles nodded. "That is a common one."

"What's your one again, Charles?"

He stared into the hissing fire. "Death."

His reply left them in silence, the five-lettered word cutting deep. If the men didn't return with help, perhaps a difficult choice would have to be made…

⌒

The fire had long gone out and a dark gloom hung over the site. Their sullen moods were compounded as they watched Charles attempt to get it going again. He did his best, but it was useless. Tom, for all his anger and threats, had a trick for getting the tinder going, and he couldn't recreate it. The constant downpour didn't help, and they all had no choice but to just sit there, soaked and depressed, trying to ignore the continuous whir of the cameras zooming in and out above them.

With a frustrated roar, Carol grabbed one of the stones that circled the fire, sprang to her feet, and launched it into the trees. A sharp buzzing came from somewhere beyond the branches.

"I hope you didn't hit one of them," Charles remarked. He didn't have to say the words, but his fear of infraction was obvious.

"Well, I fucking do," she yelled. "I hope I smashed one of those beady bastards to bits."

"Okay, my dear, that's enough. Calm down."

"Calm down? They're lucky I don't burn this forest to the ground." She made her way over to the trees, shouting into the vast nothing. After all her energy had depleted, she slumped at the base of a tree and began to cry.

Charles took off in the direction of the noise, hoping Carol didn't incur an infraction. After working his way through some of the thick foliage, being careful where he stepped, he came to what he assumed was Carol's stone. It had rebounded of a structure – a wooden shack – well-hidden from the campsite behind the mass of low branches. With caution, he ventured towards it, inspecting every detail. The door was ajar and a putrid smell cloaked the area. It reminded him of an expression his wife used: *Curiosity killed the cat*. But this didn't deter him from pushing the door open, its old rusty hinges screeching as the interior was revealed.

He buried his mouth and nose in the nook of his arm as the stench assaulted his senses, waving away a cloud of flies buzzing past him. A latrine. And by the looks of it, it had not been used or cleaned in some time. The lower part of the walls were covered with dried excrement. On the ground, in the centre, were four large holes. Each one filled to overflowing with dried faeces. He stepped back out, took a couple of refreshing breaths, then re-entered. To his left, a rod or pole, clearly an unblocking tool, probably for the use of previous participants.

Holding his breath, he took the pole and plunged it into one of holes. The crust cracked and the pole slid in and hit a hard surface, possibly plastic piping but he couldn't be sure, and there was no way he was investigating further. The stink was overwhelming, and he had to retreat retching and gagging. He shoved the door closed, still coughing up bile, and made his way back to camp.

Before he stepped out of the trees, he decided to keep his findings to himself. The smell alone would be enough to trigger Stacy's horror of germs. At least the rain helped with the smell, though he couldn't get it out of his nose. As he looked around at the remaining members, it was obvious that tears and depression dominated the mood. He took a moment to take it all in, then sank his head into his hands and silently prayed for the men to return with the news that a way home had been found.

EIGHT

Without warning, the tall pines disappeared to reveal a vast flat, snow-covered landscape stretching out to the horizon. The four men stopped in their tracks and tried to comprehend their location. The laws of nature appeared to be broken, with logic and reason going out the window at what they were witnessing before them.

"Well, one thing is for certain, lads," Tom said with a laugh, "we're not on any of the British Isles anymore."

"Where are we?" Ian asked, his voice sharp with worry and fear.

"We're a long way from home, Dorothy. How the hell should I know, mate, I didn't design this place." Tom gave the lad a withering glare. "I'm more worried about the fact that it's snowing out there and raining in here."

Richard looked around him. The stream had vanished beneath a layer of snow. Tom was right, again. It seemed like two different worlds coming together at the edge of the forest, only joined by the electric fence that ran off into the distance. Rain filtered through the trees behind them, while beyond lay an arctic wilderness that seemed to have no end. However, that was before the group noticed the dark smoke rising in the distance. And out of nowhere, the rank smell of death filled the air.

"Mother of God," Richard gasped, the stench instantly reminding him of the poor souls they'd seen fused to the perimeter fencing.

"Where to now?" he asked Tom, assuming the man had a plan, considering he'd taken on the role of mission lead.

"Your guess is as good as mine, mate. Without proper equipment, we wouldn't last half a day trekking across that, and I don't fancy seeing whatever's creating that smoke, either. The fucking smell is unbearable."

A gunshot echoed in the distance and the bark on the tree beside Richard burst into a cloud of splinters and dust.

Nabil stepped behind a tree. "Quick, take cover." But the others just stood and looked around, until another shot cracked from deep within the woods, and this time the ground at Ian's feet erupted.

"Run!" Tom roared. "They're fucking shooting at us. Watchtowers. Over there." He pointed at a dark structure in the distance.

The four sprinted away to their right, back into the woods. More shots followed, with bullets whizzing past heads, trees splintering, and dirt popping up from the forest floor.

"Keep moving," Richard shouted at Ian, his voice shaking as he raced on.

They reached a gully and took cover on the bank of the stream, all panting, eyes sparked with adrenaline as they looked about for the unknown. Tom and Nabil scanned the trees for a potential threat chasing them down.

Richard did his best to calm Ian, whose eyes were wide with shock.

"This crazy Host bastard has gunmen out there," Nabil said.

"We're f...fucked," Ian stammered, standing up and holding his chest with both hands as he hyperventilated. "How...are we going to g...get out of this?"

"Chill out, scrawny," Tom hissed, pulling him down the slope. "Just relax for a sec. They obviously want us alive. Those shots were a warning to keep us in the woods. They're gonna make us play this game, whether we like it or not."

Tom's grim assessment went unchallenged.

Infractions will not be tolerated – those words came to Richard as he lay in the ditch wondering what the repercussions of their actions would be.

He picked splinters from his shoulder, thankful it hadn't been his eye, both of which he closed now for a long moment as he accepted that they had no choice but to head back to camp. Damn it, but with only rags for protection, they didn't stand a chance against the frozen wilderness beyond the woods. Unbearable cold, electric-perimeter fencing, and now gunmen off in distant watchtowers. There was only one way out of this place alive, and they all knew it.

NINE

Tiff looked on in awe as Charles shared stories of his life back home – about his deceased wife, who he loved so much, and about his grandchildren. She couldn't understand how he remained so calm in this dire situation. He was so positive and, when she engaged in conversation with him, it transported her away. But then reality hit and she worried that he wasn't with them at all, considering what he was saying and what was going on around him. *Maybe he's a bit cuckoo because of his age?* But she liked him nonetheless – the grandfather she never had – and he was keeping her spirits up while they sat in the horrible rain, which refused to stop.

She looked over to Stacy, who was struggling to deal with everything. The poor girl – fear anchored her to her bed, praying for rescue to come and get her out of this place. All she did was lie there, staring with blank eyes into the dead fire pit. Whatever hope she'd harboured had faded in the watery haze that danced in front of her.

The sombre mood and silence in the camp shifted at the sound of people approaching. Everyone jumped up, apart from Two, their eyes wide in a mix of fear and hope, not knowing if it was their captors or rescue. Then the four men stepped out of the forest, tired, hungry, scared, and soaked, like them all.

"They're back!" Tiff cried, her voice laced with hope. But her enthusiastic welcome was met with silence. The news wasn't good.

"What happened out there, chaps?" Charles asked, stepping forward.

None of them could look him in the eye. Eventually, Richard revealed the news about the armed watchers at the edge of the woods. Escape was impossible, and real fear hit home in the minds of all – this game had only begun and it wasn't just the four returnees who would have to play, it was everyone, and they were going to have to participate whether they liked it or not.

❧

Days dragged by without any sign of a break in their routine, with life in camp turning into a boring cycle of never-ending waiting. Long periods went by without anyone talking to each other, with everyone anxious for the Host to deliver an objective that might bring them closer to getting home. Richard didn't believe it was going to be that easy.

At the crack of dawn, an alarm would go off and they'd all have to stand for roll call. The Host would call their number and each would respond out of fear of infraction. Everyone except Two, on whose behalf Charles spoke. After attendance was confirmed, the cameras buzzed as the Host demanded their cutlery be cleaned and presented for inspection. Daily rations would be dropped through the canopy, consisting of a bottle of water to share between the nine of them, basic vegetables for soup, and a small loaf of bread, which they all kept for the evening – sometimes the following morning.

Charles spoke about how they were being conditioned, with every passing hour seeing a piece of their dignity stripped away. Richard admired the man for his efforts at keeping morale up, but understood how difficult it was for him.

It took enormous work to get the fire going again, and once it was blazing they huddled round trying to get some warmth into their bodies, even pulling Two closer to help her catch some heat. No one spoke, though Richard knew they all harboured similar thoughts as they stared into the dancing flames: what was going to happen after their failed escape attempt? It had been days now, with no word of what the punishment would be.

Broken rules in Block 18 would not be tolerated – the consequences of which he couldn't comprehend right now.

The pole with the speaker shot up from the ground, its silver coating reflecting the flames. They all stared at it, but no static hissing or struggle to find the correct tuning came this time, just a hive of whirring from the cameras above. Something was coming. The sense of anticipation was palpable around the fire as they awaited the next transmission.

Then the speaker crackled.

ATTENTION, PARTICIPANTS.

OBJECTIVE ONE DEADLINE BREACHED DUE TO INFRACTION.

INFRACTIONS WILL NOT BE TOLERATED.

NOTIFICATION OF RULE BREACH ISSUED TO SUBSCRIBERS.

PENALTIES WILL APPLY TO ALL PARTICIPANTS.

Richard looked around the silent group, catching what he thought was an accusatory eye from Stacy and Carol. *What the fuck? What where we supposed to do, just sit and let this shit come down on us without any kind of protest?* The men had only gone because they were the strongest. Well, not so much Ian, but his determination had won the day – if anything had been won. No one was here of their own volition, and certainly no one wanted to stay.

PENALTY: PROVISIONS SUSPENDED.

SUBSCRIBER STATUS: DISSATISFIED WITH BLOCK EIGHTEEN PROGRESS.

COMMENCE SURVEY...

RETRIBUTION FOR RULE BREAK TO BE ACTIVATED IN ONE HOUR.

An ominous silence ensued, where everyone looked an unspoken question at each other: What the hell was going to happen to them?

The speaker crackled again.

SUBSCRIBER STATUS: SURVEY RESULTS COMPLETE.

PENALTY RETRIBUTION: THREE FINGERS FROM ONE PARTICIPANT.

IMPLEMENT FOR OBJECTIVE WILL BE PROVIDED.

REWARD: REINSTATEMENT OF PROVISIONS.

FAILURE TO COMPLETE OBJECTIVE: ONE PARTICIPANT WILL BE SELECTED FOR EXECUTION.

PARTICIPANTS HAVE ONE HOUR TO COMPLY.

The group watched in silence as The Host's transmitter returned underground. A gasp ran through them when a black-handled hunting knife took its place. Richard looked from face to face, as did most of those gathered. The instructions were crystal clear, including the repercussions if they failed. Horrific. Cameras in the trees sparked to life, their adjusting lenses buzzing like a swarm of flying insects.

"Okay, chaps, let's be logical about this," Charles said, his hand trembling as he looked about the group.

"Logical?" Tom shouted. "Are you serious, mate? You heard what he said – do this or one of us will be executed, never mind starving to fucking death."

"I know, I know. Please calm down. Surely we must all be prepared to let the hour go by without hurting anyone."

His words were met with an eerie silence. Everyone looked down at the dirt.

"I don't know, Chucky," Tom said. "If the objective is going to be physical, I'd rather have something in me going into it."

Carol jumped up. "Surely you can't be serious, Tom?"

"I fucking am, love. I'm as serious as a heart attack."

"Charles is right. If we all refuse, they'll see how strong we are when united."

Tom snorted. "And you're willing to test them? Look at us. Look what they've already done. They've gotten in our heads. Injected fear. All the while subjecting us to these conditions. And we've just begun this crazy shit."

"And I suppose you're going to be the one who is going to do it, then?" Tiff said.

Tom folded his arms across his chest and glared back at her. Then he looked from one to the other. "Am I the only one seeing what's going on here? I'll be fucked if I'm going to live out my days in the belly of a leper playing happy families."

"No, Tom, you're not," Richard said. "You'll forgive us all for not being eager to chop one-another up. I vote to go hungry. They'll never kill us. Whoever the fuck the subscribers are, they want us alive for their entertainment."

"Ah, great idea, my boy." Charles clapped, his eyes beaming.

"What is?"

"A vote would settle this silly argument once and for all. We shall do a *yay* or *nay* and let that be the end of the discussion. Nothing like a bit of good old democracy to settle an argument."

They each used a piece of charred firewood to mark the inside of their hands with the letters Y or N. Two was exempt from the vote due to her inability to communicate, but it was decided that if the vote was tied, her fingers would be taken.

"Ok," Charles said. "Let's get on with it, shall we. We will go in order." He revealed the palm of his wrinkled hand – No.

Nabil was next up. He threw Tom a glance as he revealed his vote – Yes.

Tom nodded his approval.

The group turned to Stacy. She didn't hesitate in showing her hand – Yes.

Carol tutted and looked at her in disgust.

Next up was Ian – Yes.

"Have you all gone mad?" Richard shouted.

Ian shrugged. "Better than being executed, Richie. Charles is right. Voting on it is the civilised way to determine things."

"Civilised? But—"

Charles hushed him and turned to Carol. Her no vote brought a smile to his face.

"Richard?" Charles said, knowing the answer – No.

"Okay, ladies and gentlemen, we are tied at three apiece, and I think we know what Thomas has on his hand."

"That's right, old man, I'm saying *Yes*, and I'm doing so because it's right for the group. I'd sacrifice three fingers over eight or nine hungry bellies any day of the week."

Charles sighed and shook his head. "Okay, that leaves little Tiff with the casting vote, so I suppose, and I am ashamed to have to do this, but we shall have to move on and figure out who's going to do the necessary on Two."

The group whispered among themselves with possible ideas. Nabil and Tom were eager to get on with it, while Carol scoffed at Stacy over her vote.

Ian sat in silence in the middle of the clamber and Richard watched them all, amazed that they were faced with such an horrific dilemma in the first place.

"Shut up!" Tiff cried. "All of you, just shut up." She glanced about the group. "There's no need to talk about this anymore."

"And why's that, love?" Tom asked, looked down his nose at her. "Daddy can't buy you out of this one."

Tiff opened her hand to reveal a black Y, which was met with a gasp of disbelief. "My father is dead. And I can make my own decisions, you judgemental asshole."

Tom, for the first time, was stuck for words, obviously shocked that the little girl of the group was able to stick up for herself.

"You can't be serious, my dear?" Charles said, his eyes wide, mouth agape.

Tiff got to her feet, her shoulders squared. "I want to go home, Charles."

"But, Tiffany, there are other ways."

"No, Charles, fingers or death – they are the only two choices we have, but I'm not going to take advantage of Two, the weakest member of our group." She rubbed tears from her eyes. "Time to get real, and why are you getting on my case? Four others voted the same and I don't see you saying anything to them. So, just… back off, will you."

Charles gawped in silence as Tiffany stormed off into the shadows beyond the treeline.

Richard caught the look of satisfaction in Tom's eyes. No surprise, the man was prepared to go to any length to keep himself strong, and that included not losing any fingers. Five had voted yes, and that block included Tom and Nabil, two of the strongest in the camp. So, who would it be?

"Fucking democracy, eh, Charles?" he said as he stared into the fire.

Charles remained silent for a long moment, then released a long sigh. "I believe you are correct in this case, Richard. I am normally a man of principal, respecting people's opinions, but I am afraid we have walked ourselves into the worst possible scenario."

"We sure have." Richard got to his feet. "Ok, folks, now what's the story? You've all decided, so any idea whose fingers are going to provide us with tonight's rations?"

A cacophony of voices answered, with everyone trying to talk over the other. Except Tom, who stood alone, seemingly happy to wait for everyone to sort it out among themselves.

"We should vote again," Tiff shouted, having returned from the woods.

"This isn't fucking Brexit, love," Tom said. "The results are in and it's time to choose. We're running out of time here. How about we just use the old woman over there? None of us know her and she's as good as dead anyway."

"Yeah." Nabil said in agreement.

"No chance you pair of fucking barbarians." Richard shouted, "The vote was five to three. She was excluded as soon as Tiff opened her hand. Have you got any shred of human decency in you?"

"Richard's right." Tiff added, "It's up to the eight of us now to figure this out."

Nabil went silent, while Tom scoffed and sulked.

The most acceptable solution came from Charles – a game of Rock-Paper-Scissors, only in reverse, with the winner losing his or her fingers.

The eight of them would be paired off and play the first-to-three. Then the same for the final four and, finally, the last two would play each other, with the winner the one who would *Take one for the team.*

One by one, they drew who'd face one another from a pile of sticks, with the one short twig used each time to make the match.

Tom was up first against Nabil, and won three in a row, much to his dislike, sending him into the next round.

Charles beat Tiff, and Richard was eliminated by Ian.

Carol took pride in losing to Stacy.

In the final four, Ian took on Charles and, despite his best efforts to lose, he won, advancing him to the final match.

Tom, hesitating, called the game into question, but the group overruled him. He beat Stacy with three straight wins and went forward to play Ian in the final match.

Charles clarified the rules for the final – the first person to win three games sacrificed their fingers. The group reluctantly agreed, then gathered round.

Everyone except Nabil rooted for Ian to come away with his hand intact. Tom won the first round and let out a roar of frustration. Then he stepped up to Ian. "If I lose my fingers to you, you little runt, I'm going to make you fucking eat them."

The camp went silent as the second round took place. Their hands bounced three times in front of each other, and on the final turn, Tom chose rock and Ian opted for scissors.

"I say, Thomas," Charles said, "you are looking a bit nervous there."

Tom's lips thinned, but he ignored the comment and instead glared into Ian's eyes. They went again and Ian pulled one back. Sweat dripped from both men's brows. A whisper of *C'mon, Ian* travelled through the air. They went again – two to two.

Tom punched the air. "Yes! Fucking c'mon. Right, Ian, mate, let's do this…"

Both men clenched their fists, brows furrowed with determination. They threw out their knuckles, and after three shakes and the unlocking of their fingers, the result was in. Ian chose scissors, while Tom chose paper.

Ian crashed to the ground in despair, and Tom celebrated as if England had just won the World Cup. "Get fucking in!" He fist-punched the air each time he shouted it.

Tiffany ran to Ian and wrapped her arms around him.

Tom clapped with excitement. "Unlucky, Ian, mate. You thought you had me there. But, hey, at least you won two of the rounds, eh?"

"Oh, shut up and sit down," Richard barked.

Tom turned and squared up, his eyes gleaming with an adrenaline high. "What's that, mate? You gonna volunteer for him, then, are you?"

Richard didn't relish the prospect of fighting. Tom's mindset was easy to read, even in the fever of victory. The bastard was in this to win, at any cost.

Charles stepped forward. "Gentlemen, let us be adults here. Savages, in fact, but adult savages." He drew an outstretched arm across the gathering. "It has been decided. Let us get on with it."

Ian shoved Tiffany aside and took off running towards the trees.

His actions prompted Tom and Nabil to sprint after him. Richard followed, but kept his distance, watching as the two men chased Ian down like hounds after a fox. As they caught up, Nabil clipped the back of Ian's heel, sending him into the dirt face first, his momentum driving him into a tree, opening a gash above his left eye.

"No point running, mate," Tom said as he leaned his knee on the back of Ian's neck, "this is happening!"

He jumped up and Nabil grabbed the young lad beneath his armpits and hoisted him to his feet. Blood trickled down the side of his face.

"Please, don't do this," he begged, his voice cracking as he was shoved back towards the camp. "Richie is right, this is madness. Please."

Tom pushed him. "Shut your mouth. And fuck Richie. Keep going or you'll be dragged back."

Richard stayed behind a tree and let them pass without comment. He made his way around the camp and entered unseen, joining the group as they watched Ian being dragged up beside the fire.

The hour was nearly up and the overhead branches buzzed as the cameras sparked into life again.

They were watching.

Tom grabbed the knife and held it against Ian's neck. "Stop your moaning. Be happy that your sacrifice will save someone's life."

All sorts of heroic notions swarmed through Richard's head, but his energy was sapped, and he wasn't about to go up against that knife. Not yet, and not without support. As it was, everyone seemed transfixed, just staring in horror at the bloodied and cowering Ian, the blade hovering close to his throat.

Tom called out to The Host and announced that the decision had been made. The speaker didn't rise, but the cameras whirred and shifted.

Ian squirmed as he was pushed onto his knees. He begged for help, pleading for them not to do this, but nobody moved, and his cries went unanswered.

Tom grabbed Ian's wrist and pressed his hand against the ground. "Stop struggling, boy. Now, take a deep breath and let's get this over with."

Ian blubbered and cried, his whole body shaking, with snot bubbling from his nose.

Tom ignored the cries and handed the knife to Nabil, who stared at it, as if in shock. "Come on, mate, I'm holding him still. You have to do it."

Nabil's mouth opened, but no sound came out.

The camp remained quiet.

"Richie? Help me, Richie. Please!"

Richard's gut twisted as Ian howled, but he remained silent and still. What the fuck could he do?

"Nabz, man, just fucking do it."

Nabil stiffened, as if he'd been slapped. He looked around the gathering, the vein in his neck throbbing, his chest heaving as the pressure reached boiling point.

"Nabz, for fuck's sake, just do it!"

The muscles in Nabil's face stood out as he gritted his teeth and stepped forward. Ian's harrowing screams reverberated through the camp as the knife sliced across the young man's fingers. The sharp blade did its job well, with blood bubbling and squirting from the open wounds. The penance was paid.

Tom released his grip, the separation of the bones forcing him away, retching, as did several others.

Ian howled and rolled on the ground, clutching his mutilated hand. Richard ran to him, gripped his wrist, and shoved his hand into the embers, evoking another scream from Ian and shocked protests from many of the others.

"Richard, old boy, what the hell are you doing?"

He released Ian and stood back. "What, Charles, do you want the lad to bleed out?"

Charles stared at Ian's cauterized wounds, then nodded as he realised what had been done.

Richard rubbed the back of his hand where his hairs had been singed. Any sense of civilisation they'd retained had descended into chaos. Madness. Humanity had deserted Block 18, sending it into a downward spiral of depravity, its participants' collective acquiescence justified by the prospect of food. If anything good came out of it, at least no one had died. Not yet.

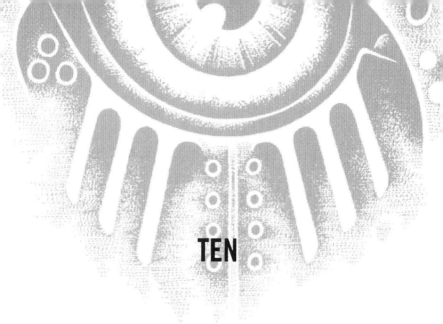

TEN

Richard sat by the stream, gazing at the water's gentle flow while he replayed the previous night's events over and over in his head. The guilt ate at him. He should have stopped it, or at least tried. And later, he should have rejected the food. It wasn't the usual mundane offering, either: a leg of lamb – not the best cut he'd ever seen, but decent enough to bring back memories, like his mother's Sunday dinners. They boiled it and shared it out the best they could – the smell almost making him float away with nostalgic reflections of better days.

When the piping-hot meat appeared in each bowl, not one of them could resist the temptation to tuck in like a savage. As he ate – the taste, the smell, the juices swirling in his mouth – he simply didn't care. If heaven had a taste, it had surely washed around his mouth, igniting every endorphin in his body into rapture. But as soon as he'd finished, he listened to his stomach battle with the sudden onslaught of solid food, and the guilt came flooding back.

He could have stopped or tossed the food aside in protest, but he'd done neither, and the thought of his cowardliness gripped him and dragged him into a dark place he didn't want to be. Earlier that morning, he'd snuck away, not failing to notice how soundly the rest of them slept, envying their guilt-free slumber. No doubt their full tummies helped. Maybe fatigue got the better of them, too? Understandable considering the trauma and stress of witnessing poor Ian being mutilated. He looked at the knife he'd taken with him. Ian's dried blood still stained its blade and hilt.

The morning air carried a hard chill, and he shivered as goosebumps popped up all over his arms. The sharp smell of damp filled his nostrils. Everywhere was wet and musty, but at least the rain had held the frost off – about the only positive he could think of. He closed his eyes and shook his head, battling against the visual of Ian's three fingers being sliced through. It wasn't just that horrific event – everything that happened since his awakening had led him into the deepest despair he'd ever experienced. His options were simple: black and white – to continue without hope, or to block it all out, permanently. There could be no life without hope.

He examined the knife. It was a precision blade, most likely used for filleting meat. With a small amount of pressure, it would slip down his arm and open his veins. What would the cold of steel entering his body feel like? Could he do it without blacking out? What was the alternative? This forest? Block 18? A decaying labyrinth of pine, and what it had to offer: fear and despair, and the deep dark unknown.

And the group. Tom. He thought back to when he'd first got to know the man. No matter the environment, his alpha-male ego superseded any sense of compassion, or the simple concept of doing the right thing. In their nightmare scenario, his will to control shone through. Richard didn't have the strength to take that battle on. Not after witnessing Ian's horror. How could walking onto a snowy field be punishable, and the removing of fingers for the sake of food not? If only he could hold The Host accountable. If only…

No, there was no hope. They would be used and abused until they either killed each other or ran through the snow hoping the gunman was on form. Or march to the perimeter fence and grab hold? Viable options all, but none of which could help him here and now. Guilt ate at him and he felt a slow death of bleeding out was the only fitting punishment – everything else was too quick and cowardly.

The blade's tip opened up the top layers of skin along his arm like a hot knife through butter. Blood welled from the wound and ran towards his hand, dripping between his fingers. He switched the knife to his bloodied hand, gritted his teeth, and ran the tip down his right arm.

There, it was done. Or, at least, he hoped so – he wasn't too sure if the method was correct. Should he have gone deeper?

He lay back and let out a long sigh, watched it all in his mind's eye, seeing himself from above, his limp body on the riverbank. Blood pooled in the dirt, then etched out a trail as it flowed into the water – a red swirl making its escape from the forest prison. But something forced his attention back and his consciousness rose from the dark depths of release. This wasn't the right way. He couldn't give up. There had to be a path through his despair – his sense of hopelessness.

He sat up and watched the blood drip off his fingers. *Fuck it, I'm not giving up. I'm going to get out of here, one way or another.*

ATTENTION: PARTICIPANT SEVEN.

A faint robotic voice called from the trees behind him.

Richard pulled himself to his feet, his scalp prickling, his mouth dry. "Who's there?"

WARNING: PARTICIPANT IN DANGER.

ATTENTION: NOW.

It was The Host, sounding an alarm, transmitting from a small speaker attached to a tree.

Richard stiffened as a cold wave washed over him. *Fuck! A man can't even kill himself in private in this godforsaken place.* He should've known. Every move he made, someone was watching. "Why don't you just kill us all and get this shit over with?" he shouted at the speaker.

PARTICIPANT NUMBER SEVEN: YOU ARE IN BREACH OF PARTICIPANT HEALTH REGULATIONS.

BLEEDING MUST BE STOPPED.

RETURN TO CAMP. ASSIST OTHER PARTICIPANTS.

FAILURE TO COMPLY WILL RESULT IN INFRACTION.

"Infraction? Come off it, you sick fuck. I don't want anything to do with these stupid objectives of yours. Either let us all go or just kill us already.

It's fucking pointless." He gripped his wrist, wincing at the pain that shot up his arm.

PARTICIPANT SEVEN: WARNING ISSUED.

COMPLY: OR SANCTIONS WILL BE ENFORCED.

"Oh, yeah? What's that then? You gonna take away my designer rags? Ha, fuck you. And my name is Richard – I'm not a fucking number."

PARTICIPANT SEVEN.

INFRACTIONS WILL NOT BE TOLERATED.

RESULT: YOUR WIFE, ELIZABETH, WILL BE ENGAGED AS PENANCE.

That stopped him dead in his tracks. The silhouette became clear – Elizabeth's beautiful face greeting him with a smile and a set of eyes that could pierce his soul at a glance, while melting his heart at the same time. The reason he'd relocated to England. For her, and her alone. For their marriage. Their future together, their happily-ever-after. Every single memory he had about her and their relationship flooded back, as if uploaded by a high-speed data port.

"You bastards!" he screamed. "Don't you dare even speak about her." He punched the tree numerous times with both fists, his knuckles bursting on impact, blood flowing from the flayed skin.

A long silence ensued, broken only by his heaving breath.

PARTICIPANT SEVEN: WARNING ISSUED.

PENANCE: COMPLY OR PAY.

The Host's transmission ended with a beep. The threat triggered a rage in Richard that had him rip the speaker from the tree and smash it against the trunk until it shattered into nothing more than a few clumps of plastic.

Elizabeth – he couldn't shake the thoughts of her as he picked himself up from the forest floor, his knuckles and arms a bloodied mess. He rinsed the blood off his hands the best he could in the stream, wiped them in his rags, and tucking both of them into his armpits, and returned to camp to find the campmates sitting around the speaker, waiting for The Host to broadcast the latest announcement.

Tiffany beckoned him, a gesture he received with gratitude. He sat next to her, noticing the blank stares from most of the participants, probably still affected by what happened the night before. He revealed his arms, catching the group's attention, which prompted Tiff to mouth to them that she was *on it.*

"Are you okay?" she whispered.

"Yeah, I'm fine," he replied, turning his hands for a quick examination. "They'll scab over with a bit of pressure."

"Here, let me take a look."

"I said I'm fine," he snapped back, his raised voice catching the attention of a few others. As a distraction, he tossed the knife down beside the fire.

Static from the speaker pulled their focus back to it – a signal that The Host was about to speak.

PARTICIPANTS: PERFORMANCE UPDATE.

POOR.

SPONSORS: DISAPPOINTED.

SUGGESTED RESULT: LOWEST RANKED PARTICIPANT TO BE NOMINATED.

DEMAND: UNPRECEDENTED.

STATISTIC UPDATE IN PROGRESS.

AWAITING RESULT…

The camp sat in silence, exchanging nervous looks at each other.

PARTICIPANTS: INDIVIDUAL PROFILES UPDATED.

RESULT: COMPLETE HISTORY, INCLUDING FAMILY AND MEDICAL.

REMINDER: PARTICIPANTS WERE NOT SELECTED AT RANDOM. PARTICIPANTS SELECTED BASED ON MENTAL ASSESSMENT.

TARGET: PHOBIAS. EACH PARTICIPANT MUST FACE AN INDIVIDUAL FEAR.

Silence. The cameras in the trees buzzed and whirred. Interest was piqued for the next part of the transmission. Phobias? Objectives based on their fears. Richard scanned the faces. To some, it seemed to make sense – to the rest, it compounded a genuine terror, evident in their eyes as they looked inward at the fear lurking within.

OBJECTIVE: THE HOLE.

PARTICIPANT: NUMBER FOUR. YOU HAVE BEEN SELECTED FOR EXERCISE.

COMPLY: OR PENALTY.

The camp turned in shock to Stacy as The Host delivered instructions about the objective. In one hour, a red flare would shoot across the sky, a signal for Stacy to leave camp and follow it to where the task would take place, with Richard assigned to walk her to the site.

After the speaker lowered, Carol went to offer her comfort, wrapping her in a gentle hug. "You'll be okay," she said. "It'll be okay."

Richard wanted to tell her to shut up. How could she know it would be okay? Like the rest of them, she had no idea what the objective involved.

"Why is it called The Hole?" Stacy asked the group, visibly perplexed with the madness of the situation. "It obviously means I'm going underground, or something, doesn't it?"

"It certainly sounds that way, love," Tom said. "But, you know, we're all in this game now and we've all got to eat. So, you know... No pressure."

"Shut up, Tom," Richard snapped. "Just...shut the fuck up!"

Tom shot forward and pressed his forehead against Richard's. "What you say, mate? I'm getting fucking tired of being the only one taking this shit seriously around here. You all think we're mates here on a fucking holiday, playing happy families?" He turned to face the rest of the group. "Well, that is not the case. This isn't fucking

Disneyland. I'm cold, hungry, and I want to get out of here."

Richard stepped away and sat back down. Weakened from blood-loss, physical confrontation was the last thing he wanted at this moment. His head spun. Maybe later.

Tom stormed off into the woods, followed by Nabil a few moments later.

"He is right," Charles said, breaking the awkward silence. His statement caught most by surprise. "I am serious, chaps. He may be rough about it, but he is right in the fact that we are all prisoners here. And I think you all know what I mean by that. So, it is either start competing or die." He shook his head and sighed. "This is all so pointless. Believe me, I would much prefer to be back in England sipping on a cup of warm tea over a few broadsheets."

The group discussed how they should proceed. They seemed to be siding with Charles, who then suggested that if they all couldn't leave or win, then perhaps it was best if they got together and ended this game themselves.

"Tom would never agree to it," Carol said.

"No, my dear, I fear you are correct. But seeing as we have descended into the murky depths of human nature, we would have to agree to solve the issue of his one-man crusade among ourselves."

The sky lit up with a red glow, which receded to a red flash that travelled across the sky like a meteor, leaving a smoky trail in its wake.

"You know what, Charles?" Richard said, getting to his feet. "We're not going to do it your way. We're going to play this game and we're going to do our best. We all have homes and families to go to, and I certainly don't want to die in this miserable shithole."

Charles stood staring at him. Richard shrugged. The poor guy was a physical wreck – basically skin and bone, his face sunken and his eyes bulging with the strain of it all.

"Sod it, old boy, you are right. Fight, eh? Yes, fight, or die trying."

"It's the only way," Richard said, turning to Stacy with his hand held out. As soon as he took his first step, he collapsed. Carol raced over to examine him, letting everyone know that malnutrition, blood loss, and everything else had caused his system to crash.

"Get him some water," he heard her ordering, though her words echoed through his head.

They fussed over provisions while Carol dressed his wounds. Water was forced into him and slowly things cleared, though his head spun. The headache that dug into the back of his skull was more intense than ever. In his mind, he battled the notions of fight or die, but the fear of Lizzy out there somewhere forced him to his feet.

Determined now, he shrugged Carol off and offered his hand to Stacy. "Come on, girl, I'll walk you to The Hole."

ELEVEN

Richard and Stacy followed the smoke trail across the sky. It led them to a part of the woods that was thick and unforgiving, and they had to work hard to get through the mass of branches and keep the flare in sight. Despite the biting cold, perspiration ran freely and their rags were soaked in no time. Richard tried in vain to wipe the stinging sweat from his eyes, but eventually gave up and just shook it off when it became unbearable.

The walk took them almost an hour, and shadows merged into permanent shade on the forest floor as the sun started to set.

He reckoned the objective would be an elaborate set-up. Perhaps with a professional television-production crew, with lights and cameras everywhere, ready to broadcast Stacy's efforts. Then they arrived and any previous assumptions vanished in the stark reality that met them.

They stood in a small clearing, bare except for a covering of dried mulch across the forest floor. However, they knew they were in the right place when cameras buzzed in the trees around them. Then The Host began speaking, but his voice was too faint, coming from the other side of the clearing. Richard guided Stacy forward, until they were close enough to make out his words.

It was definitely him. No mistaking that harsh accent.

The transmission sounded different this time, like it was in sync with their actions, not a pre-recorded one like they'd all heard back in camp.

PARTICIPANT: FOUR.

OBJECTIVE NAME: THE HOLE.

RULES: OVERCOME YOUR FEAR OF GERMS.

PARTICIPANT: PROCEED INTO THE HOLE – A TEN-MINUTE TIMER WILL BEGIN ONCE INSIDE.

PENALTY: MUST BE PAID FOR FAILURE TO COMPLETE OBJECTIVE.

OBJECTIVE: REPEL ALL ELEMENTS BASED ON YOUR FEAR.

COLLECT THE SILVER TOKEN HIDDEN INSIDE AND PLACE IN THE BAG PROVIDED.

SUBSCRIBERS: A LARGE AUDIENCE ARE FOLLOWING YOUR PROGRESS. DO NOT DISAPPOINT.

Stacy turned to Richard with a look of sheer terror. Then the ground opened a few feet from them, like a panel sliding across to reveal a pitch-black rectangular hole.

Richard put an arm around her shoulders. "Come on, Stacy. You've got this. Just focus. Think of the food and power as you go through whatever it is down there. We won't escape from this place if we are all weak and helpless. We need the nourishment. We need to be strong."

Stacy remained silent. Her breathing came hard, with sweat running down her face. He couldn't tell if she was determined or terrified. Either way, she had to be led to the entrance, shaking. A cold, putrid breath from deep inside the shadowy void rose to send an icy shockwave up his spine. He knew it would be the same for Stacy. One thing was for sure, he was glad it wasn't him going down there. Tight, dark spaces were not his thing.

"Wish me luck," she said as she took the first step into the murky depths.

He swallowed back the tightness in his throat. "Good luck. You've got this."

❧

Stacy bent and felt around for the bag. When she touched it, she grabbed it up and slung the loop around her wrist. Six steps down, she had to get onto her hands and knees, cringing as she touched the damp, sticky floor.

Breathe easy, Stacy, breathe easy. It's just a silly trial. As much as she tried to convince herself, it was easier said than done and her breath came shallow and fast as she inched forward to navigate through the dark tunnel that led down into the earth.

She crawled along, constantly feeling ahead, unable to see a thing. Then a small row of lights snapped on and lit up the tunnel ahead. *Oh, sweet Jesus. What the hell is...?* She had to squint at the glow, blinking hard to accustom her eyes after the pitch darkness.

The ground became muddier as she progressed, and the stench grew stronger – incomprehensible – almost what she imaged death would smell like. *Keep going, Stacy, keep going. It's only a ten-minute trial. Where is the token?*

When she rounded a bend, she came upon a chamber. The room was big enough for her to stand, which she did, taking time to examine

everything around her. The floor was dark –
muddier than the tunnel, and as cold to the touch.
She looked up and spotted two vents on the
ceiling, each covered with old wire mesh, with
dirty brown water dripping from both. The place
stank of... *shit* – that's the only word that came to
her as she fought hard not to vomit. The walls
were a light brown – like caked mud, or... Her
breath caught when she noticed something etched
on the one to her left.

> IN THE SEWERS
> DARKNESS FESTERS
> HOPE IS ALL YOU HAVE
> IF YOU DRAIN YOUR FEARS...

*Sewers? I'm in a sewer? In a forest? Oh, sweet
Jesus, no.* Her toes curled at the thought of what
she might be standing on, and she had to cough
out a lurking gag in her throat. If she started
vomiting, she'd never stop. She remembered she
was against a timer, but couldn't figure out what
she had to do. Then something clattered above
and behind her. A steel sheet dropped across the
tunnel, blocking any chance of escape. But that
was nothing to what came next – a gushing noise
filled the room, growing in volume until the
ground shook and a double waterfall of brown
liquid cascaded from the vents. *What the hell?* It
swept across and around the space in expanding

waves, crashing against each wall and soaking all in its way, including her.

There was no escaping it. All she could do as it rose was stand back against the metal sheet – the only surface not covered with rot. Her absolute fear of germs froze her in place as the fluid built up around her. The stench of shit and piss was so intense, she had no defence against its effects and puked the previous night's meal into the mire. As she snorted and coughed the bile out in an effort to catch a breath, the swirling torrent took her feet from beneath her and she went under, her scream cut off by a mouthful of sewerage. The taste and texture was so foul her throat spasmed and she was convinced she was about to die, choking and gagging as the current dragged her around in a blind panic.

Then reality struck. She had to get above it. If she didn't, there was no hope of survival. She kicked with all the energy left in her and broke the surface, realising when she shook the filth from her eyes that the gap to the ceiling was critically small.

She used her arms and legs in a frantic effort to stay up, the gap diminishing until she had just enough room to keep her mouth and nostrils free. "Help! Somebody get me out of here? Help me!"

Nobody was coming. Richard, so close, would have no idea what she was going through. If she didn't do something about it, she would die in this chamber of faeces. She took a deep breath and let the current take her, kicking off a wall to propel herself deeper in an effort to search for something that could help.

She opened her eyes, but visibility was minimal. All she could do was reach out and kick until she connected with a wall, feeling along until she touched the floor. But she couldn't go any further. She had to get air, as foul as it was. Otherwise her lungs would explode and she would die. Simple as.

With her heart pounding through her head, she kicked up with all her might and banged her head off the ceiling, but she had just about enough room to breathe, holding on to one of the vent grills to stop the current dragging her under. On the second plunge, the current proved too strong for her to remain in one spot for long enough to explore. Panic gripped her again as her chest tightened under the immense pressure, and she was convinced it would implode and cave in on her. She had to get air.

As she prepared for the third plunge, she knew it would be the last one. If she didn't succeed, she would surely die, for the gap to the ceiling was almost closed. She sucked in one final breath and propelled herself down, keeping her eyes open as she let the current take her around the room. There had to be something. Why the hell bring her in if there was no hope? Then, as if out of nowhere, she remembered the final words some poor soul etched into the wall. *Drain your fears. Drain your fears!*

A visual of her as a toddler in the bath flashed across her eyes. She used to request the stopper be yanked while she stayed under to watch the bathwater flow down the drain, kicking against the current, knowing her parents got great amusement out of it, too. Little did she know those childish antics would someday prompt her to do something that could save her life.

She kicked and fought against the current and forced herself onto the floor, crawling along as she dug her hands into the muck. *Time is running out, Stacy, time is running out.* Chunks came loose, but all she could feel was tiled flooring. At least she'd got to that. Her lungs ached from the pressure, screaming for air. *No more time!* Then her fingers grazed something different – round – possibly the top of a rubber stopper. She pulled at the shit and dirt until she felt the round stopper, all the while struggling against the current.

With her last vestige of strength, she gripped the ring and pulled it out. The suction was instant and she braced herself with legs apart as the sewerage rushed from the chamber. But she couldn't wait. She powered up, screaming inside against the maddening urge to suck in anything to fill her strangled lungs. *I can't hold it. I can't hold it!* As she drove up, she opened her mouth –

she couldn't help it – and gawped, just as her head broke the surface. A mix of rancid fluid and air raced into her lungs, but it was enough to pull her body off the edge. She coughed and gagged, then sucked in another lungful, her feet hitting the floor as the liquid level continued to decrease. She thought her head was going to explode with the pressure as she choked and spluttered between each panic-filled breath. Then something flashed, catching her eye, and she screamed as she dived into the remaining sludge to grab the silver token. Her fingers touched it, but the current had it and it pinged off the portal and disappeared with a sucking sound that felt like her whole being was being pulled into the end of the world.

She ended lying exhausted on the filth-covered floor, shaking all over, gasping for breath and retching in equal measure, snorting and coughing to clear her nose and throat. The worst thing was her inability to rid her mouth of the taste. It filled her in the most horrific way imaginable. But, in reality, the worst thing was the vision of that silver token vanishing into the darkness. *Why didn't I see it? Why didn't I grab it?*

A voice broke the silence, but she had to shake her head to clear her ears and make out what it was saying. It was calling her number, and sounded like it was coming from one of the vents. She knew without doubt that it was The Host. Any hope she had that she'd done well in simply surviving and could return to camp to sleep was dashed when the voice told her she'd failed the objective and an extreme penance would have to be paid. With that, she just gave up. Better to be dead.

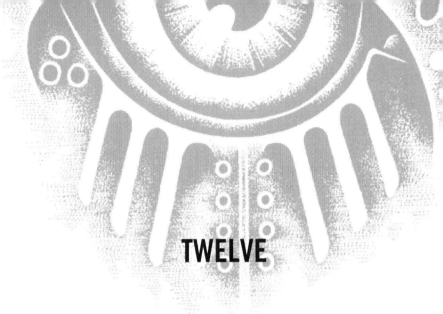

TWELVE

Block 18 was a relatively peaceful place after darkness fell and this night was the mildest since they'd arrived in camp, with the rain finally stopping and the frost staying away. Participants had the opportunity to dry their bedding and clothing, and although they went to bed hungry, for the most part, they slept soundly.

Stacy's failure was not begrudged.

At first, Tom was angry that the camp would go without decent food, but when Richard returned with the broken woman held underarm, any festering resentment dissipated.

Stacy was visibly shattered, physically exhausted, and drained of any sense of inner strength. If Richard hadn't held her up, she would have collapsed in a trembling and incoherent heap. The woman had, for all intent and purpose, given up, and was now nothing but an empty shell.

Carol and Charles put her to bed straight away and tried to comfort her, but their compassionate efforts to coax her back into the real world were wasted.

Richard could only impart the sparse details Stacy had mumbled when she'd crawled from the tunnel, covered in shit and stinking like a sewer. The camp were aware from The Host that she'd failed the objective, but they saw from her condition that her efforts must have taken her beyond her strengths. Whatever happened down there – the exposure of her darkest fears – had more or less broken her mind and left her almost comatose.

The scene was too much for some. Richard needed space and leaned against a tree on the fringes of the camp, staring off into the dark woodland. A little earlier, he'd seen Tiff and Nabil making themselves scarce, too. He hadn't expected to see Stacy in the state she'd appeared in. Now that he thought of it, he hadn't known what to expect. Any notion of decent food, or even the penalty to come, disappeared at the sight of the poor woman and her deepening torment and depression as he'd struggled to help her back to camp. *What a day.* He needed sleep if he was to continue tomorrow with any chance of surviving. At least the rain had held off. With dry bedding, a decent sleep might be on the cards. He needed to make the best of it because he had no doubt time was running out for them all.

With the fire's flames still licking at the darkness, it didn't take long for him to slip into a deep, dreamless state, until the camp was awoken with loud screams and horrific moaning. He shot up and looked around to hone in on the sounds. Others seemed to be doing the same, but with the screams echoing off the trees, and the place in darkness, it took a while to figure out.

Campmates called out, asking to see if anyone knew what was happening.

Carol rushed past Richard and stopped at Stacy's bed. "It's not Stacy. No change from earlier."

"Over here," Charles shouted. "Come quick."

Richard ran over – number Two was awake. When he looked at her leg, he had to turn away to avoid the stink. *Fuck!* That smell could only mean one thing – infection had set in so deep the pain had become unbearable. The poor woman howled and screamed, and despite Carol and Charles' best efforts to comfort her, she seemed to get worse with every passing second. The more they tried, the worse she reacted. She flung herself off the bed and twisted and rolled around the clearing like a woman under demonic possession. Richard grabbed and held her head as firmly as he could. It was all he could do to prevent her ending up in the still-hot embers.

"Shut her up, will you!" Tom shouted, clearly affected by the woman's agonising screams.

Charles and Carol ignored him as they helped Richard corral Two away from the fire or from smashing into beds or trees.

Tiff, on the other hand, slapped Tom and demanded he shut up.

Tom shoved her away, marched over to the campfire, and removed one of the circle stones.

"Wait!" Tiff cried. "What are you doing? Tom? Tom!" But her words fell on deaf ears and Tom continued forward. With one strike, silence returned to the camp.

The woman with the number two carved into the back of her head lay motionless on the forest floor.

Richard couldn't move, shocked to his core at what had just happened. Tom stood over her with the stone still in hand. He looked around and shrugged. "Someone had to do it. She should have been put out of her misery the first day she got here."

"And who are you to play God?" Charles asked, his chest heaving.

"What do you propose, Chuck? We're in the middle of this forest with nothing but a few rags. That woman needed a hospital and the fucking talking pipe over there was never gonna let that happen."

Richard gritted his teeth, fists pressed against his thighs. The bastard was proud of what he'd just done. The alpha-fucking-male had just sorted out their little problem.

"We'll bury her somewhere in the morning," Tom said, his voice softer as he placed a hand on Charles' shoulder. "It's all we can do, mate."

With a cough that sounded more like a loud bark, Two sparked into life again. This time foam spewed from her mouth and her body went into spasm, the whites of her eyes showing as they rolled back into her head.

"She's still alive, you idiot," Carol screamed. "Do something."

Tiffany turned away and buried her head in Nabil's chest. He embraced her, but it couldn't block out the woman's awful groans.

"Do something, Tom," Charles demanded. "Come on, man, move."

Richard fought back a raging desire to roar at Tom's seeming inability to act. The man was frozen to the spot, his eyes wide as he stared at Two twitching and squirming on the ground. He mumbled something, but all Richard could catch was – "I...can't." *Well, I can.* He ran behind the group to the campfire, found what he needed, and made his way back.

Carol and Charles had given up trying to calm the woman – there was nothing to be done – she was uncontrollable, gagging and convulsing in the dark, on the verge of suffocation. Richard knelt beside her and lifted her head and shoulders so she lay against him. Everyone stood back, frozen in shock, until Two's strangling cries and groans faded to a low gurgling – then silence. It was obvious that the woman's misery had ended.

They didn't look at Richard as they focused on each other, no doubt with an uncomfortable mix of sadness and relief. Two's head rested in the crook of his elbow, the cold steel of the blade lying across her throat, hot blood pouring from the gaping wound and across his lap.

Carol and Tiff cried when the awful reality registered.

"Richard, no!"

He got to his feet with the knife held tight, then walked over to a slack-jawed Tom and stared him in the eyes. "You want to control everything around here, but when the going gets tough, you're nothing more than a bottler." He looked him up and down. "Her blood is on your hands... Mate." He gripped Tom's wrist, placed the bloody knife in his hand, and walked away into the pitch black beyond the trees.

THIRTEEN

The frost came during the night, so sudden it felt to Charles as if someone had pushed a button. As a result, the ground hardened to the extent that the task of digging became a near impossibility. Instead, Two's body had to lay wrapped in rags where they'd placed her in the forest, not too far away, but out of sight. The group argued about the morality of the situation, but without the right tools, giving the woman a burial was simply not going to happen.

The mood in camp had become so depleted, no one could lift their heads from their collective depression. Even when the silver cylinder rose from the ground to deliver its latest transmission, everyone just sat where they were and barely listened to the robotic words.

PARTICIPANTS: ATTENTION.

The Host's tone seemed to be growing more determined as the days wore on.

PROGRESSION: FAILURE TO COMPLETE OBJECTIVES HAS BECOME A CONCERN.

SUBSCRIBERS ARE WORRIED ABOUT DETERIORATING HEALTH LEVELS.

"Oh, fuck your subscribers!" Tiff yelled at the inanimate object.

PARTICIPANT: THREE...

BASED ON CURRENT HEALTH STATUS YOU HAVE BEEN SELECTED FOR THE NEXT OBJECTIVE.

REWARD: ADDITIONAL FOOD AND HEALTH SUPPLEMENTS.

PARTICIPANT: THREE...

BASED ON PROFILE. FEAR EXPLOITATION IS A CERTAINTY.

Charles saw that Nabil was visibly shaken. Fear exploitation could only mean thing – his worst nightmare... Snakes. The transmission provided the trial's location. No one in the group commented. Spirits were low all around, leaving Nabil to make his way into the forest alone, though Charles made sure to wish him well.

The remaining campmates slowly came to life and began the ritual of preparing the basic provisions of vegetable soup, bread, and hot water that had appeared for them that morning. Though bland and boring, all agreed that it had to be eaten, being just about enough to sustain them.

Everyone hoped Nabil would return victorious, and all fantasized about this feast they'd been promised. Their collective desire for the comfort of hot savoury food almost made them forget that they were here against their will. Almost. What if he failed? Another night without food before sleep, with only a small portion of stale vegetables to look forward to the next morning. Between their malnourished state, losing Two the night before, and their constant struggle to remember their past, it wasn't surprising the general mood was so dark. Most of them didn't care anymore, and Charles worried about that. They needed hope if they were to survive this place.

He looked over to Stacy's camp bed. She was the only one who hadn't got up, still lying motionless beneath the pile of rags they'd covered her with the night before. While the group ate their meagre rations, he got up and walked over to her, his heartbeat thumping in his ears. Something wasn't right. She was normally the first one up, bedding hand-washed and neatly folded. He'd hoped her horrific ordeal wouldn't get the better of her after a night's rest – that she'd wake up and be stronger for having come through it. But she'd taken it hard, there was no doubting it. Maybe food would help.

As soon as he touched her, he knew. Even through the layers of ragged cloth, she was stiff and cold as ice. Frozen. He shook her in the hope that he was wrong, but there was no arguing the reality. What lay on the bed was dead weight.

"Oh, no. Stacy. You poor, poor woman."

He pulled back the rag covering her face to reveal dulled eyes staring up at him, her expression blank and lifeless. As he brushed his fingers across her cheek, his mind raced back through the darkness of his past, filling him with a pain he'd never wanted to experience again. He remembered the morning he woke to his wife lying next to him, cold, stiff, and lifeless, like poor Stacy. It was without doubt the darkest day of his life, even compared to this current nightmare. He could never forget the look in his sweet darling's eyes. As if she'd known – had tried to connect with him as her breath left her for the last time – a lingering hint of the pain and realisation that came to her in the moment, while he'd slept. It was a look he carried with him from that day onward.

All he could hope was that she hadn't suffered, that she'd simply slipped away.

A hand on his shoulder took him out of his past. Richard hunkered down beside him, shaking his head in a slow manner as he released a long sigh. "I thought this might be the case when I noticed you here, Charles. Fuck. This hellhole is getting grimmer."

Charles stood and turned to the camp. "My friends." He took a deep breath. "I am afraid I have bad news to impart. Stacy has left us for a better world. May God have mercy on her soul."

Carol rushed over and ran her hands over Stacy, frantic in her efforts to find life. She pulled the rags down and recoiled in horror at the mass of frozen blood that covered Stacy and her bed.

"No!" Her cry echoed around the camp, lingering as she raised her face to the canopy. Charles held her, his hold gentle as she sobbed. It was then he noticed the wounds on Stacy's arms, and the knife beside her hip.

Richard and Carol followed his gaze and Carol pushed away from him and ran up to Tom, screaming as she clawed at his face.

"You did this, you horrible man. You did this, didn't you?"

Tom stood strong, arms up – boxer style – to block her slaps and punches, as if allowing her time to vent her anger and frustration on him. Then, without warning, he stepped to his right and punched her in the side of the face, knocking her to the ground.

"Enough!" he roared, backing away. "Now stay the fuck away from me. All of you." He held his arms out, pointing at them all. "I had nothing to do with this."

"I gave you the knife," Richard said, stepping past Charles, who had bent to assist Carol. "What did you do?"

"Nothing, and don't go accusing me of something that crazy bitch did to herself."

Carol nursed her cheek and glared at him. "You saying she did it by herself?"

"That's exactly what I'm saying. We all saw the state of her after that objective. She was covered in shit and her fucking mind was gone."

Charles stepped towards him, unable to control his anger and disgust. Poor Stacy, lying there, staring into the afterlife, just like his darling wife. "Handing someone a knife, Thomas, is just as bad as doing it yourself. Why didn't you help her?"

"I was asleep, Chuck. Don't you start accusing me, too. Kooky bitch took it while we all slept."

"Stop calling her names!" Tiffany shouted.

"I'll call her whatever the fuck I want, Babes." He looked around. "Seriously, am I the only one seeing things for what they really are here? You all want to play happy families? Is that it?"

Richard stepped past Charles. "No one is asking you to stay, so why don't you fuck off and go it alone?"

Charles touched Richard's elbow to encourage him to step back, but Tom swung a left hook that caught him smack on the jawline. Richard stumbled back, and Charles braced himself to catch him, but the man regained his balance and shot forward with what could only be described as an arcing swing, hitting Tom low in the ribs. Tom bent to absorb the impact, but only for a moment, gipping Richard's arm and dragging him to the ground where they grappled and grunted while trading punches.

Charles and Tiffany tried to pull them apart, but the violence of the tussle proved too much for them and they were forced back, leaving dust and dirt flying into the air along with snarls and expletives from the wrestling men. Even Ian, with his useless hand, tried to intervene, but Carol pulled him back to prevent further damage.

After what felt like forever, but in reality was only about thirty seconds of frenetic brawling, Tom gained the upper hand on an energy-sapped Richard, pinning him to the ground with one hand and delivering a flurry of punches that busted his nose and opened his left eyebrow. He finished his assault with an elbow to Richard's temple, knocking any semblance of fight out of him.

Tom sprung up, a bloodied and beaten Richard at his feet, and screamed a tribal-like roar that echoed through the camp. The remaining campmates stood back in clear astonishment.

"Now listen here, you fuckers." He took several deep breaths as he looked everyone in the eye. "I'm willing to be violent to protect myself and get out of this fucking hellhole, but I'm not a killer." He coughed hard and spat into the dirt. "If I could have helped that girl, I would have." He ground his teeth, then shook his head and walked off into the woods.

FOURTEEN

Nabil made his way through the forest, following the flare each time it was sent up. His clothing, or the rags that constituted such, were soaked through with sweat, even against the freezing air. While weak and tired, he was grateful that the mysterious subscribers had selected him, giving him a break from the awful monotony and recent horror of the camp, but also a chance to prove himself. He just didn't like the idea of there being snakes involved. Or at least that's what he was gearing himself up to face.

Damn it, if I can win this task, eat some decent food, then I may be in a position to push on and find a way out of this nightmare. This thought drove him forward, past the hunger and the tiredness, but not the growing unease at what slithery things might lie ahead.

The final flare landed ahead as he approached a clearing. In front of him stood a huge brown-coloured box, like one of those forty-foot shipping containers you'd see down on the docks, only this one was made from wood. A sheet with what looked to be instructions was posted on its door. The task was simple, in theory: Go in, collect the silver token, and the camp would receive provisions. Nabil didn't want to waste time pondering the possibilities, but he couldn't banish that warning voice niggling at him. What lay ahead? He knew his goal – his mission – but he feared there was more to it than simply grabbing a token.

He pulled the door open and cringed against the unmistakable stench that took him straight back to the nightmare he'd spent years burying. Memories stirred, taking him back to a night he wished he'd stayed at home. It was supposed to be the biggest and best night of his life – the highlight of his career – but it ended in a pool of blood, sweat, and tears.

In Britain, he was touted as the next big boxing sensation, and he rode that wave, demolishing all contenders on his way to the top. When he finally got his shot at a world title, defeat was simply not an option. The bell rang, he stepped forward, staring the champion, Nathaniel Johnson, in the eye. However, before he found his trademark rhythm, all he could remember was the sparkling lights dancing above his laid-out body. The crowd reacted with hateful, adrenaline-fuelled screams, as a flurry of trainers, referees, and media officials gathered around him. But within the swirl of pure chaos, among the frenzy, a moment of clarity etched itself forever into his mind – Nate 'The Snake' Johnson, a fellow Mancunian, stepped over him in what seemed like slow motion, green-serpent emblems glittering beneath the houselights on his black boots and trunks, and walked away with his trademark, arrogant, snake-like swagger.

Nate's actions sparked a reaction from Nabil's corner and a brawl broke out. During the melee, from somewhere in the crowd a snake was thrown into the ring, landing beside Nabil's head. In his daze, he struggled to comprehend what he was seeing and before he could react, the panicked creature unleashed a flurry of strikes to his face. He retreated away from the animal into the corner of the ring. Clutching his face, terrified, he cried into his gloves. The chorus in the arena grew into a hysterical hissing that overwhelmed him, plunging him into a shadow realm he thought he'd never come out of.

Snakes. Fucking snakes.

He took a steadying breath, closed his eyes, and stepped inside the box, inching the door closed behind him. It clicked shut, with more than one latch engaging, and he found himself enveloped in complete darkness. All he could hear was the sound of his own breathing beneath his heartbeat thundering through his ears.

While he waited, catching his breath, his nostrils stung with the smell – one he could never forget, even if he lived to be one hundred. Then every follicle shot to attention as an ice-cold shiver raced through him. *That noise.* He swallowed hard, his throat parched dry. It was the same noise that had kept him awake every night after the title fight, shivering beneath the duvet, remembering... Unmistakable, feeding his ultimate fear. The slither. The hiss. The knockout. Every possible element associated with the reptile now acted as a psychological weapon against his ability to think clearly, and he was not alone in this box. Then The Host's voice crackled from somewhere lost in the dark.

PARTICIPANT: NUMBER THREE.

OBJECTIVE: TWO MINUTES HAVE BEEN ALLOCATED TO COMPLETE OBJECTIVE.

PENALTY: FAILURE TO COMPLETE OBJECTIVE WITHIN ALLOCATED TIME WILL RESULT IN PERMANENT LOCKDOWN. YOUR CAMP WILL NOT RECEIVE PROVISIONS AND PARTICIPANT WILL BE ELIMINATED.

OBJECTIVE: SILVER TOKEN MUST BE COLLECTED AND PRESENTED TO THE CAMERA AT THE DOOR TO SUCCESSFULLY COMPLETE OBJECTIVE.

SUBSCRIBERS: VIEWERSHIP COUNT IS HIGH FOR LIVE OBJECTIVE.

BUFFERING EXPECTED.

ROOM WILL BE FILLED WITH MANY DIFFERENT SPECIES OF SNAKES AT SUBSCRIBER'S REQUEST.

NO LIGHT IS PERMITTED IN THE ROOM DURING THIS OBJECTIVE.

OBJECTIVE: BEGINS AT THE END OF THIS TRANSMISSION.

The transmission ended with a beep. Then silence. Nabil froze on the spot. What could be more extreme than being trapped in a dark box with…? His senses went into overdrive as he tried to gain control of the situation, but the fear ate into him, and all he could think about was snakes. Then the sounds came to him: Slithering, hissing – buzzing cameras, and a timer beeping somewhere in the darkness.

He wiped his sweaty palms against his loincloth, then stepped forward, tipping at the cold steel floor. That was good. If he could feel the floor, it was clear of... He pushed the word out of his head and growled to clear the nervous tension from his throat.

The box, wooden on the outside, was steel inside. Solid. He hadn't seen one like this before, and he'd been around. A forty-foot container should only take him thirteen footsteps to reach the end. Thirteen. Not so bad. Twelve now that he'd taken the first. But that sound. Even with the pitch black, he kept his eyes open. He took another step, slow and meticulous, as if moving through the noise and smell of his unseen foe.

No, not foe. There was more than just Nate in with him. Foes? There had to be hundreds with the amount of slithering and hissing, getting louder and closer with each step. But there was no going back. No escape. The space was alive, with the constant ticking behind it all.

He shivered again as he imagined the walls having scales and pulsating with life, but despite the occupants, he couldn't help but imagine Nate's slick bobbing and weaving, seconds away from laying him out. Heat filled his head as his heart thundered. *Please, Nabil, do not faint. All will be lost. Move forward. Get to the end. Escape.*

ONE MINUTE REMAINING.

Panic gripped his chest, each breath shallow and fast. *Where is that token?* He almost fell as he finished his next step, the sole of his foot landing on his worst nightmare – slithering scales. The unseen serpent shifting across his path, its hiss filling every part of him. He gritted his teeth against the desire to cry out. *Stay with it, Nabil. Eight more steps.*

Was the timer picking up pace?

This time, he led with his toes – his weight on his back leg – testing the space ahead, listening, sensing. It didn't matter, though, because the room was alive now, with dark movement all around him. Something touched the back of his foot, his ankle, and he leaped into the air, praying that he wouldn't land on one of the demons. In that airborne split second, fear clawed at him, robbing him of whatever control he'd gathered. He would take a dozen of Nate's punches on the chin over the thoughts of being trapped in a tomb full of serpents.

He landed with horror on a thick, writhing body and fell hard onto the steel floor, whimpering and thrashing about as a veritable sea of snakes coiled around his legs and arms.

"No!" he screamed, beating and kicking them away, scrambling up and holding his hands out, hoping beyond hope that he was going in the right direction. *How many more steps?* He'd lost count.

The timer racing down now. More contact. Crushing coils around his leg. He beat and punched the beast, pushing with all his might until it released its hold. Another step, evoking a cry of relief when his hand collided with a wall. He'd made it across. Or had he? Was it the right one? No time to waste. He began searching, running both palms across the ridged surface, all the while kicking at anything that slithered. Then it was like all the good and positive things in the world came to him when he touched a loose piece of metal on the floor – his ticket to freedom. It had to be.

"Yes!" His heart filled with equal measures of relief and delight, but the celebrations were short-lived at the unmistakable sound of latches releasing, not beside him but at the other end. He turned to see a sliver of light entering the space as the door he'd come through opened a finger's width, revealing the horror lying ahead of him, curling and coiling across the floor. As the light spread, more snakes came into view. The Hosts voice boomed.

THIRTY SECONDS REMAINING.

"No!" Nabil roared, squinting as he adjusted to the light. He leaned back against the wall, groaning as his heart raced beyond belief. They thought they had him beat, but they didn't know how tough he was, having grown up in a council estate in Manchester, or how hard it was to be a Muslim kid during a less than understanding time. Despite his fears and constant exclusion, his determination not to be beaten propelled him and turned him into one of Britain's finest boxers – a national hero to some. A man you didn't want to cross. Now he'd been crossed, and they would not beat him.

It was with this mindset that he took his first step back across the snake-infested room. With the token clutched in his hand, he placed his foot on the floor, continuing to feel for slithering life. Then yellow light filled the space, so bright he had to shield his eyes. When he took his hand away, he nearly choked at the shock of what lay ahead. The floor was a mass of twisting, coiling life, with hundreds of the slithery ophidians scrabbling for space.

TWENTY SECONDS REMAINING.

As he tried to gather his thoughts before moving through the scaly sea, he noticed there were dozens of different types of reptile. The constrictors gathered mostly at the walls, flickering out their tongues as they responded to the light. He didn't pay much attention to them, aware that they normally attack from above. The problem he faced was the huge king cobra that rose up before him, its eyes locked on his. Its intent was clear – it was going to strike.

He glanced about for an escape, but there was nowhere to go. The thing was huge, and no matter where he went, the cobra could strike him.

His only option was to make a run for the door. The cobra raised itself to his height, waiting for him, its eyes reminding him of Nate's look milliseconds before he ate the canvas. Then the idea came to fight fire with fire. Snake against snake. Well, in a way. Reaching down, he lifted a manageable constrictor by its tail and swung it with all his might at the cobra. The two snakes tangled and he rushed down the side of the container, using squirming snakes as a platform when he had to.

TEN SECONDS REMAINING.

Fuck! Not far now. He was almost within reach when something stung his right calf and the most intense sensation he had ever experienced shot up his leg.

"No!"

Then the same thing happened to his other leg. This time heat surged through him like a wave of fire, burning every nerve-ending and pulling him to the floor amid a scene that matched his worst nightmares.

Without the strength to lift his head, he didn't have to look down to know one of the vipers had done a job on him. However, as he lay on the floor surrounded by a massing nest of snakes, he couldn't help but notice the beady black eyes of the biggest one in the container. An anaconda. Its brownish scales and black patches gleamed beneath the lights. A natural object of pure power. His heart lurched when the mouth opened and moved over his feet, which he couldn't move, its muscles clamping around his ankles as it made its way up his legs, swallowing him inch by inch.

FIVE SECONDS REMAINING.

The timer seemed to take forever between beats. The venom was fast-acting, paralyzing him to the extent that he could only release his hold on the silver token. As the timer counted down, in his head all he could hear were the numbers shouted by the ref as he counted him out of the fight. Today would be no different, which he found ironic. The knockout seemed like a distant tickle in comparison to the horrific sensation of being consumed. Something pulled him back from the door, but he couldn't move his eyes to see what it was. Then he was pulled again and he knew the anaconda was making good progress as it worked its way up his body.

FOUR.

His bones cracked.

THREE.

His inner scream was only heard by him.

TWO.

His eyes, on the verge of popping, rolled back into his head.

ONE.

Blackout.

FIFTEEN

I don't care what you say, Charles, I'm out of here. I gave him the knife and he let this happen. If I see his face again, I don't know what I'll do." Richard grimaced as Carol and Tiff endeavoured to clean him up. Both his eyes were swollen, his left brow stinging and still bleeding from the many punches he'd received.

Charles tried his best to calm him, but Richard wasn't having it. He wished he had the strength to follow Tom down to the river and force the bastard's head under the water and watch him drown. But instead, the guilt burned into him for not keeping watch over the knife. It was as much his fault that Stacy was dead as Tom's. Things were going from bad to worse, which gave him good reason to take his chances against The Host and attempt another escape – by himself this time. Ian would be a hindrance, and Nabil hadn't returned from his objective.

The campmates weren't happy and tried to convince him to stay. Perhaps because he was the only one now who could physically stand up to Tom, even if he had suffered a beating at his hands. But he didn't care anymore, and nothing could make him change his mind, so he prepared to head off again.

"How exactly do you propose to get out of here, Richard?" Charles asked. They all knew the gunmen would be watching the treeline and the cameras would see all and alert them.

"I'll take my chances, Charles."

Tiffany stomped her foot. "And what, just leave us here to become another victim of The Host and his subscriber friends? And then there's Tom. Who's going to protect us from that narcissistic lunatic? With no one here to put it up to him, he'll take over the camp."

Carol and Ian stood beside her and nodded agreement, but Richard just shrugged, wished them well, and headed off, determined to figure a way out of this madness, or die doing so.

❦

Snow filtered through the trees as he jogged and walked, keeping within his physical limits, only stopping to drink from the stream. He watched all around him, convinced he was being followed, but never spotting anyone to confirm his paranoia, apart from the cameras, which he was positive tracked his every move.

All he could do was press on. He still hadn't figured out how he was going to disappear from sight. When he reached the treeline, he waited for the gunfire, but none came, so he sat and watched, looking for something – a weakness that would give him a way out. The watchtowers were distant and appeared unmanned.

Hours passed, though he had no real way of telling the time. Sometimes he felt as if he was all alone, then it was like they were breathing down his neck. Even so, he continued to survey the land in front of him. Snow and ice ran for what seemed like miles from the treeline to the far off mountains. Could he do it? How many steps had they taken into the snow before the gunfire rained down on them last time? No, making a run for it was out of the question. Although, what other choice did he have? Maybe he could crawl through it, staying low enough to blend in? It might work if he ran zigzag – he'd be a harder target to hit and would cut the distance to the other side. But even if he got that far, how would he get over the fence? Dammit, it was now or never. If he stayed, he would die anyway.

He took a deep breath and stood, then leaped into the snow.

"Richard, wait!" someone called from behind him.

He knew that voice. *Fuck!* The snow was deep enough – midway up his calf, with nothing beneath but frozen grass. And cold. Freezing cold. It was a bad idea. He didn't have to think hard about that to know it. Instead, he turned to search for Ian, easily spotting him at the treeline, holding his mutilated hand to his chest.

"What are you doing here, kid?"

"Come back here. Hurry. I've to tell you something."

Richard obliged, his feet already numb. He stepped between the trees and stamped snow off. "Go on then. What's the big secret?"

Ian's eyes were wide with worry, or was it fear. Not surprising considering the shit they'd been through.

"Nabil..." he began, but choked up and couldn't get another word out.

"Go on, lad, out with it. What about him?"

Ian went on to report that The Host had informed them that Nabil had left this world and the campmates were reduced to stale soup as a result of his failure. They'd discussed the situation among themselves and he'd been delegated to follow and ask him to return.

"I'm sorry about Nabil, Ian, but there's nothing back there for me. Don't you get it? These objectives, whatever the fuck they're called, are all rigged. Pointless. This is the work of some sick bastard using us for his own twisted entertainment. And he's broadcasting it across the internet. Has to be. Probably making a killing from it. Can't you see that?"

Ian stood in silence, chewing his bottom lip, tears streaming down his face.

"Look, lad, we've two choices here: go back and wait to be called off somewhere to die, or take our chances out there." He gestured to the vast tundra beyond the treeline. "All we can hope is that we don't catch a bullet."

"What about the electric fence?"

"We'll cross that bridge when we get to it."

"But I don't want to die."

Richard sensed the dread dragging him down, but refused to start mentoring him now. Whatever hope he had that someone would help him was long dead.

He wrapped an arm around Ian's thin shoulders. "We'll wait until dark, then make a run for it."

WATCHERS IN THE DARK

SIXTEEN

R ichard and Ian gazed across the cold land as darkness fell. The sky beyond the canopy was clear and a tapestry of stars glinted against the expansive black backdrop. Both of them were freezing from the wait, but at the same time prepared to make the potentially perilous journey in the hope of finding freedom on the other side.

"What you think?" Richard whispered. "Now?"

Ian was shaking, and not just from the cold. He pulled himself to his feet. "I don't think I can make it that far, Richie. My toes are numb, and turning black, and I just don't have the energy."

"Listen, Ian, if we don't do this now, we are going to die in these woods. Whoever is running this show is not fucking around. Okay? You understand me? This is serious." He ordered the lad to count backward from ten to help compose himself.

"You can do this. Just keep your head low and follow me."

"Okay, Richie, let's do it."

They took one last deep breath and glanced at each other. Then they were off. Both sprinted forward, the fresh snow crunching with every footstep. Richard's heartbeat thundered through his ears as he fought to keep the pace up.

"Keep going, lad. Keep at it, you're doing great."

They didn't look back until forced to a slow jog by sheer lack of energy and deepening snow. When they stopped, they hunkered down so they wouldn't stand out. As each struggled to catch his breath, they looked back at the dark mass of trees and saw they'd travelled quite a distance. So far, no gunshots or alarms – all they could hear was their own raspy breathing.

"We can't stay here," Richard said. "Sitting ducks. Let's get going."

"Which way? Everything's dark, even the snow. Can't even see those watchtowers anymore."

"I know, but all we can do is work our way towards the horizon, as much as we can see it."

They took off again, running at a steadier pace, but it wasn't long before they had to stop, gasping for breath and lost in the sense of not knowing which way to go.

Ian shook his head. "It's crazy. It's like we're inside a... a snow globe."

Richard let out a long sigh. *Fuck.* The lad was right. Now that the forest was out of sight, it was impossible to tell which direction they were going. Everything looked the same. Dark snow stretched into the night beneath the canopy of stars. If only he knew enough about the constellations to navigate. Should've paid more attention in the scouts. A misty wall of nothingness in every direction with that intoxicating smell of charred death in the air.

Ian nudged him.

"What?"

"Listen..."

All he could hear was his heartbeat in his ears.

"I think it's coming from that direction." Ian pointed off to his left.

Richard indulged him, squinting into the distance. The misty veil presented an object but he couldn't make out what it was.

"Fuck it, let's take a look."

They crouched and made their way towards it, their progress slow, but as they got closer it came into focus – one of the watchtowers, right there in front of them. If that wasn't bad enough, running alongside it was fencing with more fried bodies stuck to it.

Ian, however, had his attention elsewhere – voices from the path that ran alongside the tower.

Richard couldn't believe his eyes. What looked to be participants, he assumed from other blocks – easily forty or fifty of them, and all in a single row – were being processed by guards.

He pulled Ian down into the snow in a desperate attempt not to be seen. They watched the guards strip the prisoners down, blast them with water from a hose, before herding them into the back of a truck like cattle on the way to an abattoir.

"We've seen enough," Richard whispered, "time to go."

They made their retreat from the compound, staying low, when someone shouted from behind them. Fuck, were they spotted?

He looked up to see one of the participants had wrangled free from the group and taken off in their direction.

"Fuck, the bastard will lead them straight to us."

"Oh, Jesus," Ian cried, leaning against Richard and shaking as the escapee was chased down and engulfed in a steam of flames from what had to be a flamethrower held by one of the guards.

Richard listened to the poor man's screams, but they didn't last long. *At least he's free. Which way to go now?* "Come on, we have to keep moving. We have to lose them."

When he turned right, he thought he caught a murmuring, but it wasn't distinctive enough to make out. Then it came to him: More voices – men shouting.

Ian gripped his forearm and his heart leapt at the unmistakable sound of barking.

"Dogs! They know we're here." He pulled the lad after him. "Run!"

They took off back in the direction of the misty fog they hoped would take them towards the mountains. Richard didn't want to leave Ian behind, but he also didn't want to be mauled by an animal trained to attack. With almost every step, the barking and howling grew louder.

"Ahh! Richard!"

Richard looked behind to see Ian flat in the snow. Black shadows were coming their way.

"Come on, boy, get up. Come on!"

He dragged the groaning Ian to his feet and pushed him forward, but the lad coughed and wheezed as he stumbled ahead.

"Which way?"

"Forward! Just go!"

But it was too late, the dogs were bearing down on them at unbelievable speed, their snarls filling the night. Before he knew it, he was on his back with a heavy German Shepherd's jaws around his forearm. If he moved, he knew the beast would rip it to shreds.

A few feet away, Ian was facedown, a massive Shepherd standing over him, growling like something from the scariest horror movie you could imagine.

Shouts came from a short distance away and he thought he'd make a run for it himself if he could get the dog off, but the bastard must have read his mind, its grip on his arm strengthening. He cried out at the increased pressure, each tooth like a burning iron shooting up his arm.

Seconds later the night was lit by torchlight, and men in silhouette fixed their weapons on them. Richard expected the dog to be ordered off and the scorching tongue of the flamethrower to be his last memory. But it didn't come.

When they spoke, their tone was hostile and angry – possibly Russian, but he couldn't be sure. A terse command was given and the dogs released their hold and stepped back. Then he was flipped face down in the snow, his arms pulled back and his wrists bound with zip-ties – the plastic biting into his skin.

Ian cried out to him, and he looked just in time to see the lad take the butt end of a rifle to his temple. The boy didn't move after it.

"Bastards!" he roared, but his protest was met with a crunching boot to the face, rocking his head back and knocking him out.

～

Visuals came at him out of the darkness – some like snapshots, others like scenes from a film. He was with his son. The time this particular memory happened wasn't clear, but he was sure of the emotions he experienced that particular day. As the scene progressed, details filled his head. His wife was out with friends – a common occurrence since the move to London – and his son, Daniel, was alone in his bedroom.

Daniel. My dear boy, how could I have let you slip from my memory? He offered to bring the boy to a football match and the delight in the child's eyes was something he would never forget. It was a night of simple things making the biggest impacts: fast food from street vendors, an excited crowd, and a cold night full of personal warmth in Upton Park. Daniel adored the beautiful game, and that night they became confirmed fans of the club in the East End of London. They watched the claret and blue home team play well and win three points. As the players applauded their fans at the end of the game, Daniel said something Richard would never forget: "I love you, Dad." Overcome with happiness, he remembered the beauty of the floodlights on the pitch as they left the old stadium. Soft flurries of rain caught in the beam, drawing his gaze to the source, the visual blurring in the glare as he tried to regain focus.

Then he realised he was squinting into a bare amber bulb. He was on his back, not in a football stadium, and not with his son, but being transported in the rear of a truck. Beside him lay Ian, unconscious, his body jerking with every bump in the road. Tendrils of memory connected him with his son, but all vanished when the truck kicked over a particularly hard bump, sending him crashing into the sideboards. *Fuck!*

His hands were still bound. He rolled onto his side, pulled his knees up, and struggled into a sitting position. The heavy smell of death invaded his nostrils and, to his horror, he realised they were not the only ones in the back of the truck. Around them, burnt bodies lined the floor, the sight forcing him to gag and splutter, coughing bile up to clear his throat.

"Ian? Ian!"

No joy, his words fell on comatose ears. A corner of the tarp at the side flapped, and he saw through the gloom that they were heading towards what looked like a watchtower. He shifted closer, manoeuvring between the bodies, groaning at the pain in his jaw as he gasped for fresh air from beyond the opening. Ahead, a building, red brick and weather-beaten, had a spotlight on top that lit up the dirt road. Through a window in the back of the cab, he saw their captors and dogs, facing forward for now.

He made his way back and nudged Ian several times, then kicked his knee. "Ian," he whispered. "Ian, for fuck's sake, wake up." But the lad didn't budge. A trail of dried blood ran from the side of his head, caking his ragged clothing.

"Hey," he called towards the cab. "This man needs help. He's bleeding to death back here."

A small hatch in the window was drawn open and a man in a balaclava pointed a handgun at him and shouted something he didn't understand, though he assumed he was being told to shut the fuck up, or something similar in whatever language it was.

When the truck came to a stop, he looked out through the tarp and saw a dark-clad man pull a chain-link gate open.

He went to the back and saw that the compound was closed in by a tall chain-link fence, with coils of razor wire and what he guessed to be electric cables running along the top. The spotlight, with snow drifting through its beam, never took its focus off the truck.

The Host, he assumed, was inside that building, expecting his arrival. *Who else would be running the show?*

Men appeared at the back of the truck, all wearing black combat trousers, jackets and balaclavas. They dropped the vehicle's tailgate and pulled both of them out, slamming them onto the freezing concrete surface. Richard had no opportunity to get up or protest as he and the unconscious Ian were dragged by their ankles into the tower. As if the forest wasn't bad enough, he quivered at the thought of the horrors that waited inside.

SEVENTEEN

They dragged Richard down into the basement, its walls red brick, cold and unforgiving. One of the guards acted like a tour guide, pointing to doors along the way, explaining what lay beyond in broken English. A room on his right was used to house the new-born babies of female participants – where they'd be left for the rats. Another room, he referred to as *the sauna*, was used for carefully selected participants to smell wonderful things before being transported to the burning fields.

Burning fields? Richard screamed for help, but the guard mocked him with an equally wild scream in return. As he was dragged along, he couldn't help looking into the rooms they passed. It was like they'd left the doors open so he'd see what was going on. One was used to shave the heads of the participants. A malevolent barber furiously running a cut-throat razor over the prisoner's scalp, and thoroughly enjoying it by the gleeful look on his face.

In another room, an electronic needle buzzed as it carved numbers into skulls, the harsh sound accompanied by cries of terror. This combination of sights and sounds horrified Richard and had the corridor swirling in a gut-wrenching maelstrom. The place was a compound of evil, where evil men did evil things to humans. A monstrous environment used to fulfil the sick and twisted pleasures of those who paid to watch from the safety of their computers and smart phones.

The guards kicked the door open at the end of the corridor and, without saying a word, dragged him in and sat him onto a steel chair bolted to the floor in the centre of the room. Then they strapped his wrists and ankles down with thick leather restraints.

The hooded men then left and locked the steel door behind them.

Richard cried out and struggled against his bonds, but to no avail – this chair was built for purpose and would not fail. The walls were filthy, covered in a weeping grime – probably never cleaned since their construction. The ceiling, made of mouldy old oak, no doubt a witness to more atrocities than he could imagine, had one light in the middle and a dank mustiness from years of damp. The floor, grey concrete, was cold and miserable. He raised his feet back onto his heels, but his toes still ached from the bitter chill.

Sweat stung his eyes and he had to shake it away to ensure he had a clear view of the door. *What have they got planned for me?* His chest tightened as hysteria threatened to overcome him, and he had to blow quick breaths in an effort to regain control. He hated the feeling of the walls looming over him like a fucking nightmare, as if his reality wasn't bad enough.

Then it got worse when the door shot open and a man ran in holding a bucket. *What the...?* He just about had time to focus on the guy's dark eyes behind the balaclava when freezing water smashed into his face, with icy shards clattering against his teeth and eyes, evoking howls in shocked reaction.

The man ran outside and Richard managed to shake the excesses off when the brute raced back in and repeated the ice beating, sprinting out and in three more times before leaving him shattered and shocked to his core.

Strapped onto the chair, he had no way of moving or creating enough dynamic to fight off the bone-numbing cold. It ate right into his marrow, or that's how it felt, his muscles shrivelling and his heart straining as every part of him shook in mind-bending convulsions. A nightmare – one he wished he had the power to wake himself from.

The door swung open again and he braced himself for another icy onslaught, but this time the masked man brought in what looked like an old transistor radio, which he placed in front of him before leaving the room.

Even with his teeth chattering and his body screaming for heat, he managed to harvest enough phlegm and strength to spit at the device – his only form of rebellion at this point and so satisfying, even if it was only short term.

The radio sparked to life with static and muddled frequencies.

PARTICIPANT: SEVEN.

The Host began in what seemed like a live broadcast instead of the usual pre-recorded transmissions.

WE ARE DISAPPOINTED WITH YOUR ACTIONS TODAY.

THIS HAS BEEN THE WORST SET OF PARTICIPANTS IN BLOCK EIGHTEEN TO DATE.

ALL PARTICIPANTS HAVE BEEN UNSATISFACTORY AND, AS A RESULT, WE HAVE DROPPED VIEWERSHIP.

A long silence ensued and Richard didn't know whether he was expected to respond or just sit there and shiver, the latter of which he decided was the best option, simply because it didn't cause him added effort, and wouldn't get him into more trouble.

HOWEVER. ALL IS NOT LOST.

OUR SPONSORS HAVE DECIDED BOTH YOU AND NUMBER FIVE WILL CONTEST THE NEXT OBJECTIVE.

IT IS LOCATED HERE AT THE CONTROL CENTRE AND WE ARE CONFIDENT YOUR PARTICIPATION WILL BOOST OUR VIEWERSHIP AGAIN.

More silence. Richard bowed his head. *Fuck, I can't take much more of these bastards. Once I'm out of this chair, I'm going to end it once and for all. They won't win.*

COMPLY OR PENALTY.

INFRACTIONS WILL NOT BE TOLERATED.
YOUR FAMILY DEPENDS ON YOUR SUCCESS.

"What?" Richard screamed, straining against his bonds. "What have you done with them?" With every word that escaped him, his fury built to an uncontrollable level.

The door swung open and a hooded man burst in with another ice shower, but Richard raged back, screaming and cursing until he was sure his head would explode. The man just waited until the tirade was over. Then he took the radio and left the room. As the door slammed shut, Richard could have sworn he heard laughter from the other side. When his trembling anger subsided, he noticed his wrists were bloody from his struggle against the straps. He didn't care.

"My family!" he roared, but his words met nothing but solid wall. *My family.* The thoughts of being unable to protect them left him whimpering in the chair.

EIGHTEEN

The following day, masked men escorted Richard and Ian to a swimming pool in the middle of the compound, surrounded by a chain-link fence and with nothing but overcast sky above or beyond it. The misty air still reeking of burnt flesh and human decay. Richard figured they were miles from the forest, but couldn't be certain. A thin line of snow topped the razor wire, and cameras whirred and zoomed, watching every move.

The masked men released their grip and stepped back, each arming their weapons and aiming at the participants. Richard, with Ian beside him, stared into the pool's depths. An eye-opening aroma of bleach and chlorine stung the inside of his nostrils. An unnerving silence followed, broken by static from a speaker on the far side of the pool.

The Host welcomed their live audience, then proceeded to explain the trial both participants were about to embark on.

Ian, obviously terrified, kept looking to Richard for reassurance, but he had his game face on, his gaze focused on the murky bottom of the pool, trying to make sense of The Host's instructions.

OBJECTIVE: AT THE BOTTOM OF THE POOL, THERE IS A LARGE PLASTIC MAZE WITH AIR POCKETS IN STRATEGIC LOCATIONS.

PARTICIPANTS: WILL MAKE THEIR WAY TO THE END WHERE THE FINAL PART OF THE OBJECTIVE WILL BE REVEALED TO OUR SUBSCRIBERS.

REWARD: THE WINNING PARTICIPANT WILL RETURN TO BLOCK EIGHTEEN TONIGHT.

THE LOSING PARTICIPANT WILL BE EXECUTED.

COMMENCE.

The guard's rifle-butted them between their shoulder blades. Ian collapsed into the water, while Richard dove straight in and swam towards the bottom. It was only then he realised how deep the pool was – twenty-feet easy – and the pressure on his ears sent needlepoint pains through his head, but he forced himself to keep going. As he closed in on the maze, he scanned the structure and noticed an entrance. He kicked towards it, gripped its side and looked up, straining to contain air in his lungs.

Ian looked to be struggling near the top.

Richard pulled himself into the maze and raced against a growing panic until he found an air pocket at the end of the first tunnel, gasping for breath in a space not much bigger than his head. *They couldn't make the space any tighter, could they? Bastards.*

Text etched into the wall instructed him to wait for the other participant before continuing. While he waited, it dawned on him that they weren't the first people to have been put through this game.

The wait felt like an eternity, but he took the opportunity to catch his breath and compose himself. Each inhalation told him the air was depleting. Then Ian joined him, gasping and flailing.

"Take it easy, lad. Just breathe. Look, we don't have time to talk. We have to make it through this. Once we do, we can figure out a way both of us can get out of it alive. Take a breath and let's go."

Ian glared at him, but did as he was told.

With Richard leading, they navigated their way through a twisting tunnel, until they came to a fork and he swam right, expecting Ian to follow. No time to look back – his lungs were screaming again.

About a dozen hard-fought meters on, his throat threatening to open and water already in his nostrils, he found himself in another air pocket, only this one was much bigger, enabling him to crawl into it. He coughed and spat water out and gawped in howling mouthfuls of air. *Where is Ian?* He was about to get back into the water to see where the lad was, but a speaker on the wall crackled.

PARTICIPANT: NUMBER SEVEN.

OBJECTIVE: FIND THE KEY TO UNLOCK THE DOOR AT THE OTHER END OF THE CHAMBER.

"But what about…?" That was as far as he got. The water hissed and bubbled and the space began to fill. He moved forward through the compartment, took a deep breath, and ducked under. No key in sight. He ran his hands over the floor and walls, but couldn't find anything. Something clunked behind him and he turned to see a hatch in the roof open and a few electric knifefish slither through. *What the…?* A gush of air escaped his lungs and he kicked off the floor back to the much smaller air pocket, gawping in breaths to replenish his oxygen levels.

"Fuck!" *What am I to do?* The dark-brown fish swam around his torso, but didn't seem to notice him too much as they fought among themselves. The water was up to his neck and rising. "Shit, shit, shit." Then he noticed a glint at the far end of the compartment. The key! He took a deep breath and kicked off the wall, wincing at a glancing sting from one of the fish, the electric jolt reverberating through his system. Fuck, that's all he needed – electrocuted instead of drowning.

He reached the key and untied it from the loop, then forced his way back up the tunnel towards the door, so focused that he didn't see the knife fish come at him from the side. The eel nipped at his eyelid, sending blood into his eye and a shock through his head that made his throat spasm, allowing a gush of water into his lungs. Terrified he'd drown there and then, he batted the fish with the back of his hand and swam through a cloud of red, thankful there was no vicious marine life to smell his blood. Not yet, anyway.

Convinced he only had moments left before blacking out, he shot up and flattened himself against the ceiling, chest to the plastic, coughing water out and sucking in whatever air was trapped in the centimetre of space before the tunnel filled to capacity. With the key still in hand, he let himself sink, then kicked off the floor and made a charge for the door, waving the aquatic life out of his way before reaching his target.

The key slipped in easy enough, but it wouldn't turn, and his grip on his lungs got the better of him and air bubbled out of his mouth and nose. But he held on, and when he tried turning the key anticlockwise, it worked and the lock clicked. *Sneaky bastards!* When the door opened, the tunnel shifted up and he manoeuvred himself through and located another air pocket.

As he gasped for breath, he nursed his injured eye, washing the blood off as much as he could. But it wouldn't stop so he just kept the lid closed to stop the flooding. He couldn't see anything worthwhile out of it, anyway, with everything blurred and shadowed. *Damned eel must have scratched the eyeball.*

A speaker on the wall crackled – a live feed from The Host.

PARTICIPANT: SEVEN.

CONGRATULATIONS.

WE DID NOT THINK YOU'D MAKE THAT ONE.

YOUR RIVAL PARTICIPANT WAITS FOR YOU AT THE END OF THE MAZE.

Ian, you sly one. He couldn't blame him, though, not with the execution threat hanging over them. *Time to get out. Too many close-quarter spaces to be dealing with, and these fuckers know I hate tight spaces.* And they played on that. But he couldn't let Ian win the objective – his family depended on him. He took another deep breath, went under, and swam through a series of tunnels and air pockets until he eventually reached the end of the maze.

The exit led him into a large steel room, reminding him of the inside of a submarine. He entered to find Ian waiting on the other side, blood dripping from his eye but also running down his body, though he couldn't see a wound.

A pool in the centre of the room had a silver key hanging over it. A speaker suspended from the ceiling crackled.

PARTICIPANTS: FIVE AND SEVEN.

OBJECTIVE: SUBSCRIBER RATINGS ARE CLIMBING.

CONGRATULATIONS ON ACHIEVING THIS GOAL.

REWARD: WHOEVER RETRIEVES THE KEY WILL SURVIVE.

PENALTY: THE ONE WHO DOES NOT, WILL NOT.

AVOID THE POOL IF YOU VALUE YOUR LIFE.

ONLY THE KEY WILL LEAD YOU TO SALVATION...

The transmission ended and they looked from the key to each other.

"We don't have to do this, Richie. We could protest and just drown. They're going to kill us all, anyway."

Richard agreed in principal with the young lad's words, but at the same time he wanted out of the underwater maze so bad it was eating into him. His family meant more to him than any of his campmates.

"I'm sorry, Ian, we have to do this. I need to get the fuck out of this place."

Ian tip-toed around the edge of the pond. "But, Richard, by sticking together here, we can send a message to The Host that we won't go silent and die for his entertainment. No, fuck him. Look what his games did to my hand? I'm done, Richie." He held out his good hand. "Come on, what do you say?"

Richard pondered it. He'd been through enough. His body burned from exhaustion and he wished for it all to be over. But his wife and child needed him. That's if The Host was telling the truth about them. There was no way to be sure.

"Ian, maybe you're right, but—"

The young lad sparked into action and thundered into a shocked Richard, knocking him to the floor with a sharp but effective shoulder charge. He pinned him to the ground and began throwing punches with his good hand.

Richard couldn't believe it – the quiet lad from camp had burst into life with the aggression and precision of a professional MMA fighter. But after a few seconds, he realised this worked to his advantage. After he weathered a flurry of hits, most of which missed their target, Ian was all punched out.

Out of his good eye, he waited for the opening and, when Ian obliged, he swung an uppercut which caught the young lad nicely under the chin. Ian's head rocked up and Richard flipped him to the side and took control, but there was no need to hit him – the lad had gone limp, his face wane and pale.

Then he noticed the pond was bubbling. *What the...?* Piranhas! Masses of them, and they were in a frenzy, roiling around in an effort to get the blood from both of their wounds that had run into the water. *How the hell are we going to get out of here?* He looked up at the dangling key. *Can't someone put a stop to this goddam charade?*

Zooming and whirring cameras caught his attention – all watching and waiting for him to finish Ian. But instead, he lay the young man on the floor and got to his feet. "I'm not fucking doing this. You hear me, you sick bastards? I'm not doing it."

He stood as strong as he could, still shaking but defiant and proud of his decision. Something shifted behind him and he caught movement in the corner of his good eye. Ian lunged at him, but that glimpse was enough and he sidestepped the lad's reckless attack, helping him forward with a sweeping shove.

Ian entered the pond with a splash, and before Richard could register what had happened, the bubbles turned red and horrific screams filled the air.

The lad couldn't be saved, and his screams soon stopped as the water continued to boil a dark red.

Well, Ian, you've finally escaped. He didn't waste time, leaning over the horror and untangling the key from the hook. Then he got himself across the room to the door.

He knew what would come so he stood to the side and stretched over to unlock it, the door shooting open with a massive surge of water into the chamber. The pool burst upward from the pressure change. As the deluge swirled around the room, the level rose at a rapid pace – over his knees, then up to his waist, but the current was still far too strong to get through the door. He held on firmly to the frame and to his horror, he noticed the spread of blood from the centre, which meant one thing only – those fucking fish where coming for him.

The water kept rising and he decided it was now or never. He took a deep breath and ducked under, fighting with all his might against the flow, all too aware of the rising red cloud blooming behind him. All he had to do was get through, then kick off the floor towards the surface. Lucky for him the current was keeping what was left of Ian in the chamber, so the piranha hadn't yet caught on to his escape. He pulled himself through and pushed off, his lungs screeching again for air as he struggled upward.

The light looked to be miles away, and he feared he wouldn't make it. To die at this stage, after all he'd gone through, would be nothing short of ironic. Whatever energy was left in his body had faded. The surface was close, but too far – he wasn't going to reach it. He kicked one last time, into darkness.

Then hands grasped his and he was hoisted out by masked men. He gasped for breath and lay motionless on his back, looking up at the sky. *Fuck, what now?*

NINETEEN

Tom paced the camp like a caged animal. "What's taking so long? Those two should have been back by now?" His agitation wasn't helping the anxious minds huddled around the fire.

"Shut up," Tiff snapped. "You're wrecking my head."

Tom stopped and glared at her.

"Don't you understand, Tom? Nabil's dead. And Ian and Richard probably are, too. They didn't make it. We're all fucked!"

Tom snorted and turned away, shaking his head.

Tiff lay back on her bed, sobbing. Everyone was wrecked, battling fatigue and hunger.

"Keep your chin up, Tiffany," Charles said, doing his best to keep his own spirits up as he offered her a bowl of soup. It was so difficult maintaining any sort of positivity. The daily ration just about kept them ticking over, but the mundane task of eating such a bland meal was becoming a gruelling chore. Moral had suffered a near-fatal blow with the absence of the departed campmates, and the isolation and unknowing only compounded the negativity among those remaining.

Tom, however, seemed to be dealing with it the best out of the four of them, even with his obvious frustrations surfacing every so often. He'd come over and shared some of his thoughts earlier, convinced this was all part of a test – a mental task between the remaining participants now that everyone else was gone. It wasn't over by a longshot, according to him, and he was determined not to end up like the others. He was going to make it out of the forest if it was the last thing he did.

Charles sighed and stared into the campfire. "Perhaps this is it, Thomas, my boy? Maybe it's just us four left."

"Maybe, Chuck. But it doesn't make sense. If the little eyes in these fucking trees are watching us, then it must be one hell of a boring show. Let's all tune in to watch four people sit around and starve to death? Bollocks, mate, I'm not buying it."

"Maybe the others have escaped?" Carol said, sitting up.

Tom snorted again. "And maybe pigs will fly, darling. And maybe one will fall into our laps and we'll have rasher soup over a nice cup of hot water."

Everyone sat in silence after that, until the earth cracked and the silver post rose from the ground. The Host issued another objective to the remaining participants – this time targeting Carol and, more specifically, her fear of heights. At first light, she was to be summoned towards the mountainous region beyond Block 18.

COMPLY OR PENALTY. INFRACTIONS WILL NOT BE TOLERATED.

She held her head in both hands. "I can't take much more of this, I just can't. I need to get out of this place."

"You're not facing this one alone," Tiff said.

Tom sniggered. "Oh, yeah, what are you going to do, love? Build her a set of wings."

"Oh, do shut up, Tom," Charles snapped, unable to hold himself back. "Tiffany is right, the Host is dragging us off one at a time. It is torture, and we need to work together." He looked around and shook his head. "Maybe that is the whole point of this place."

"The point of this place is redundant, Chuck. It's a sick game. Nothing more. What, you think you're in some sort of purgatory? Eh? Is this your final test before the big pearly white gates open up for you?"

"We all have to believe in something," Charles replied.

"Ha, whatever you say, old ma—"

Tiffany silenced Tom with a slap. "Enough! Seriously. Look at Carol. She's a nervous wreck. We have to support her. Help her."

Tom, rubbing his cheek, got up and walked towards the woods. "That's the second time you've done that. There won't be a third. You three go do whatever you want. I'm done with all of this nonsense."

"We could use your strength," Charles called after him, attempting to reason, but his words disappeared into the shadows with Tom.

TWENTY

Richard awoke with shock in the cellar. Ice water dripped from his face, and another masked man stood glaring at him. At least the fucker wasn't running out to get another bucketful. Richard spat out a shard of ice and coughed to clear his throat. He looked the guard up and down with his good eye. Bastard was built like a bear, wearing a black bomber jacket and combats – despite the layers, he could make out the man was in peak physical condition, aggressive and intimidating.

He glared at Richard, his eyes bloodshot and straining, as if holding himself back from an imminent attack was almost too much for him.

"If you do not like it, I can always use boiling water!" he roared, his thick Eastern European accent echoing off the filthy walls. He marched up to Richard and butted his balaclava-covered brow against his.

Richard groaned.

"You say something?" he asked, his voice high-pitched, verging on manic.

Richard remained silent. The guy's breath stank.

"I did not fucking think so." His nostrils flared, his eyeballs tracked with crooked veins – filled with a burning rage. But he didn't carry through his obvious desire to inflict more suffering. Instead, he twitched, broke eye contact, and stormed out of the room.

As soon as the steel door slammed shut, Richard exhaled a long sigh of relief. What the fuck had happened? Where was his reward for winning the trial? What the hell was Ian's death for? Obviously nothing, except to entertain their audience.

He looked around the room. It was just him now – the chair, the restraints, and fuck-all else. On the back of the door, in spray paint, letters spelling Block 18 stared back at him. Then static came from beneath the chair. He strained against his bonds, gaining just enough traction to spot the radio on the floor. As soon as he locked his eye on it, he knew what would happen. The device fizzed into life with a crackle, then The Host spoke, but the audio quality was poor and he struggled to make out what was being said. Whoever had the bright idea to place it under the seat hadn't considered the effect of a bucketful of iced water.

It wasn't long before the thing died and the room fell silent.

He hardly had time to breathe when the door flew open and slammed against the wall. Two masked men, armed with rifles, entered and bore down on him.

"You heard the order," one of them roared, "your next objective starts now."

"Wait. What? Please." Richard strained half-heartedly against his bonds – his energy zapped. "I... I didn't hear shit. What's going on? Please, I can't take anymore. Where's my family?"

The men didn't wait to discuss the matter. They released him from the chair and delivered a flurry of vicious punches and kicks to keep him in check.

Richard lay on the cold wet floor, naked, trembling all over from the beating, with a deep chill in his bones and the horrible feeling that something beyond his deepest fears was coming his way.

The men tied his arms behind his back and lifted him with a tight grip under each armpit. They dragged him out of the room, his limp feet scraping along the concrete. He had no energy to put up any sort of protest, never mind a fight. They carried him down a long corridor, into blinding daylight, and out past the pool. When they reached the end of the compound, he caught a glimpse of what he assumed was the main tower and made note of the door before the men placed a hood over his head and threw him into the back of a truck. He lay there, trembling, listening to the engine ticking over. A harrowing thought echoed in his mind: *I'm never going to see home again.*

As they took off, he put all his focus into mentally mapping the journey, assuming he was heading back to the camp, but the road seemed smoother than last time. Before he knew it, he was hoisted out and dragged along again. This time the ground was different. His feet scraped over a rough, yet softer surface, and he guessed it had to be the forest floor. Camp? Dinner? They did say a completed objective would see him back at camp. As fed up as he was with vegetable soup, he relished the prospect of slurping down a bowl now.

When they stopped, the hood was removed and he had to squint against the light, struggling to blink away the blur. They pulled him to his feet, and when his vision sharpened, he realised they were in a forest, with large pines surrounding the clearing. Then his blood ran cold. A few meters ahead was a rectangular hole in the ground, with a large mound of soil beside it. His legs went to jelly and he fell to his knees, but he was dragged back up again and held by both arms.

Beside what could only be construed as a grave lay a casket made of the same kind of flimsy wood used to transport vegetables from a truck to a supermarket.

"No. You bastards. No!" Tremors racked his body, and he would have collapsed again, if not for the fact he was being held up. "No! I won the fucking objective. You said I could go back to the camp."

The thug on his right delivered a blow to his stomach, knocking all air from him and taking him to his knees. Then, as he gasped for breath, his bonds were cut and he was grabbed by his ankles and head and slammed into the coffin.

He screamed in terror and struggled to get out, but a punch to the head quietened him enough to allow them to place the lid on top, with teasing slivers of light trickling through the slats.

"Please!" he cried. "Please. I won the objective. Get me out of here. Please! I won the fucking objective."

"By order of The Host, you are to spend six hours beneath ground."

"Please, no! This is a fucking death sentence." He banged his knees against the lid like a child having a tantrum – but it was useless. They nailed the lid shut, every thump of the hammer driving home the horror of his reality. He gagged and coughed, struggling to catch his breath as panic surged through him.

Then he was lifted, and for a moment there was nothing, as if he lay in a cotton ball, or soft cloud. But it wasn't to last – his world crashed when the coffin landed at the bottom of the hole, and any remaining light disappeared as heavy clumps of clay tumbled in on top of him, time after time – clump, clump – bearing down, with laughter from above growing fainter with each thump.

Then there was nothing but the horrific sound of his heartbeat pounding through is head, beating off the inside of his skull. The darkness consumed him and he screamed again. But no one could hear his cries. His worst nightmare had begun.

TWENTY-ONE

Beyond the forest, a snowy mountain range loomed, its ominous peaks overlooking the land. Through the middle of the range, a valley cut deep into the rock. Somewhere high between the jagged slopes, a rope bridge linked each side, often blowing violently in the constant wind that funnelled through the gorge. On one side, a starting point. On the other, an end. The objective was clear: brave the elements – cross over successfully and collect the silver token.

In theory, that seemed simple. However, to Carol, it was anything but. Her acrophobia stretched back as long as she could remember. Her counselling sessions never resolved the issue, but they did help her discover the root cause. As a child, she was hung over a balcony by her drunken father in a poor attempt at humour while on holiday in Spain. One of many incidents of child abuse she'd suffered. Her father laughed that day, but the trauma followed her ever since, and now she found herself above a gorge, desperately trying to beat her demon.

Every nerve shook as she looked down from the rope bridge into the abyss. Her problem wasn't vertigo, as much as a horrible uneasiness – a loss of balance and inner stability when there was basically nothing below her. It froze her in the past and did the same now as she clung to the two hand ropes. She kept repeating the Host's words over and over in her head: *The objective is simple: cross to the other side, collect the token, go back to camp.* Only problem was, she'd got barely halfway when paralysis gripped her.

Tiff and Charles shouted encouragement from the start point, but it wasn't working – she needed help before the blood rushing to her head blacked her out and she plummeted to the bottom of the valley.

After the Host announced the next objective and who was to undertake it, the remaining campmates, except for Tom, huddled together and tried to motivate each other with whatever spirit they had left. But Carol knew once heights were involved, she would have an impossible test on her hands. She pretended she was okay with it, managing to hide her distress behind a positive facade – a technique she was well used to using –

but the black spots that danced across her vision only increased with every passing second.

It took the three of them over four hours to reach the valley where the trial would take place. At the bottom, a gravel pit had been freshly dug. Slaves, possibly from another block – naked, chained together with their mouths sewn shut – chipped away at the frozen earth with pickaxes and old shovels. The mutes glanced upward, watched Carol struggle on the high rope bridge for a moment, then went back to work.

The lack of decent food and sleep impacted the three of them to a major extent and, by the time they arrived, their reserves were more or less depleted. Despite this, Carol soldiered on. When she reached out and gripped the ropes in each hand, she held firm and blocked out the gap between. But as she ventured out on the single footrope, her fears crept up her legs and wreaked havoc on her ability to concentrate. With every step, the rope felt a bit slacker, and the strengthening wind caused the bridge to constantly shake and wobble.

The strain increased in her arms and legs as she held on, trying to keep her balance through the shifts and swings. But something deeper than fatigue was becoming her greatest enemy – not The Host, these games, or Block 18 – something from within, both physical and mental. It overwhelmed her. She cried out as a strangling wave of panic surged through her, the grip in both hands softening as her muscles turned to putty. She closed her eyes and cried, knowing everything was lost. "I'm done!"

❧

"She's not going to make it, Charles," Tiff said, knowing she was the only one who could go out and bring her back in.

"I agree, my dear. I'm prepared to survive on shitty soup for the foreseeable."

"Hang on, Carol! I'm coming out for you." The wind took her words away, confirmed when Carol didn't acknowledge her.

With every step she took, the rope bridge shifted and swung, but heights didn't bother her.

"Be careful," Charles shouted.

"Hang on, Carol. I'm coming." But then the worst happened. Carol leaned to her left and the foot rope went right. The stretch was too much and she lost her footing, ending up hanging from the hand ropes, kicking with both legs, too weak to lift them high enough.

"Wait, Carol. Carol!" Tiff increased her pace, but the foot rope shook and shimmied so much she had to slow down.

Carol screamed and lost her grip on one rope, and Tiff held her breath, unable to move another step. Then Carol's other hand opened and she fell.

"Carol! No!"

But the unbelievable happened and she managed to grab hold of the foot rope, ending up dangling from one hand, with both feet still kicking beneath her.

"Help me. Help me!" she cried, her eyes wide with the fear and the realisation that she might be only moments from her doom.

"Hold on, Carol, I'm almost there," Tiff called, making her way along the rope. "Just a few more steps to go."

It didn't take her long, and when she arrived she reached down and grabbed Carol's wrist, keeping a firm hold on one rope. "Get your other hand up here and grab on," she shouted against the howling wind.

However, Carol was frozen with terror and Tiff's simple instructions went unanswered.

"Carol, please listen to me. If you don't do this, you're going to die. Get your fucking hand up here. Now!" Carol was moments from annihilation, and she was the only one who could save her. "Carol, come on. Please... Please!"

Something changed in Carol's eyes. She looked up at Tiff, her gaze cold and... hopeless.

"Don't worry about me, girl. I'm done with this place."

"What? Carol, no. Come on, work with me here and you'll be fine."

Tiff tightened her grip – something inside told her to – but then Carol's hold softened and her fingers uncurled one by one from around the rope, and within the blink of an eye her whole body weight was in Tiff's hand. Dead weight, pulling hard on her already exhausted reserves, her shoulder screaming out in pain from the awful strain.

"Carol, please!" Tears streamed down her cheeks until the ferocious wind whipped them away. "Carol, help me help you."

Carol maintained eye contact but hers conveyed a resignation that filled Tiff with despair. She pulled herself up and whispered softly into Tiff's ear, "Tiffany, I've seen enough to know that no matter what, we are done for."

"No, Carol, there's always hope." She gritted her teeth as the pressure increased on her arm.

"No, my dear, they've been in control from the beginning. Best to end it on my terms."

Tiff shook her head, biting back the sobs. "Please, Carol, don't do this. I need you."

"Tiffany, child, let me go. I'm okay with it."

"No, I'm not letting go. I'm not!"

Carol looked her in the eye, reached up with her free arm, and grabbed Tiff's wrist. At first, Tiff nearly let out a whoop of joy, thinking Carol had listened to her, but then horror filled her when Carol pulled her gripped arm free and, all of a sudden, she was the one holding on. But as soon as Tiff realised this, it was too late.

Carol actually winked, released her hold, and allowed gravity take her.

Tiffany screamed and reached out as Carol fell in what seemed like slow motion. She couldn't help but notice the smile on the woman's face as she went out of focus and disappeared into the gravelly chasm below.

TWENTY-TWO

For what seemed like hours, Richard screamed and cried and begged, scraping at the wood, his nails peeling and ripping until the pain and exhaustion forced him to stop. All hope of escape was dissolving but within the darkness, his madness evolved – the never-ending battle brought him around to each and every dark corner in the labyrinth of his mind. He struggled with the heightening of his senses: smell, taste, touch – the awareness of just how dark it was. Awareness of his physical form slipped away as his mind roamed free within his dark prison.

A maelstrom of colours and abstract designs flashed into focus, like an invisible artist splashing paints across a canvas, all so different – some flickering, some zooming in and out, glowing and changing, reminding him of the one time he'd seen the Northern Lights while on his honeymoon off the coast of Iceland. No one visual stood out, but the overall effect dug into the depths of his mind and soul, drawing a flurry of emotions to the surface, building to such an intensity he found himself, as if wakening, screaming and crying and calling out to his wife.

"Elizabeth!"

A sob escaped as he remembered the day something terrible happened. Elizabeth picked Daniel and him up after a disappointing night at the Boleyn Ground. The Hammers had exited the cup and the mood on the drive home was at an all-time low.

Daniel had nodded off in the back, which was when Elizabeth decided to tell him. She confessed to her whereabouts, not just that night, but nearly every time they'd attended a match. This memory felt so new, so fresh – how hadn't he remembered it? He must have buried it so deep in order to cope with the resultant trauma. As he lay in the darkness, he recalled everything, and like the opening of a flood gate, the shock, the pain, the emotions, came at him in wave after wave – so many visuals – so many questions. He cried out again, struggling to keep a grip.

Elizabeth had had enough. The sneaking around and the playing of games was all too much and she'd decided that night was the night all of it would stop.

He'd refused to believe it was happening, and they fought with a frustrated caution so they wouldn't wake the sleeping child in the back seat – his belt unbuckled so he could lay out in comfort with Richard's jacket laid over him.

"Who is he?" he demanded. Not that it mattered but at the time it seemed like the right question to ask. For a while she refused to answer. But when she did, it was like a bomb had gone off in the car.

"Tom."

Of all the people. They spent their days together, working so close for so long. How in the hell hadn't he seen it? The silence was broken by a flurry of punches to the dashboard. Daniel woke up crying out at the commotion, and that's when it happened – Elizabeth turned to calm him, her caring action allowing the car to veer.

Richard was too busy venting to see it coming. By the time they saw the truck's headlights, it was too late. The last thing he recalled was the sight of his son, in slow motion, gliding past him and out through the windscreen – the boy's face frozen with shock and confusion.

The following morning, Richard woke to find himself in the ICU section of the Royal London Hospital. The sombre-looking police officer confirmed that both Elizabeth and Daniel were dead. The realisation hit him like the crash had just happened all over again, and he cried so hard and for so long, with partial memories slipping in and out of his view, never staying long enough to grasp, but all evoking a string of harrowing sobs.

Then something crackled, dragging him out of his torment. His awareness sharpened, as if returning to the physical aspect of his being – his coffin, his predicament. Low audio came from what he assumed to be a speaker wired into the casket. It made sense. They could probably see him, too. But not his thoughts – they couldn't get in there. But they knew how to expose one of his fears, so perhaps they could?

The Host informed him that his time in the box was nearing completion, but he would remain there until his fellow participants located the grave and dug him up. His mind shot into leader-mode again. Would they even know where he was? Even if they did, the casket was buried six feet under almost frozen soil. And how much oxygen had he left? They'd placed a speaker on the box, but was there a feed for air? Had his hysterical outbursts soaked up most of it? But then much of his time had been spent deep in his mind, so maybe his body had closed down enough not to tax the system. He could only hope.

He closed his eyes and tried to focus on surviving. Now it was a battle against the clock, and he didn't know how much time was left. While his body entered a state of stasis, his mind kicked in and focused on the irony of his situation.

Tom. The bastard. Somewhere deep inside, he always knew the man couldn't be trusted. Even with his situation being so dire, he couldn't help smile at the sheer absurdity of it all. Would the untrustworthy snake and the rest of the camp get to him before his air ran out? Time would tell...

TWENTY-THREE

Breathing slow now, everything but his mind had shifted into a state resembling hibernation, his consciousness remaining active – aware – listening, and through the coffin lid and the layers of clay, it heard a voice calling his name. It wasn't the crackly speaker like before but the manic voice of someone struggling, striving – possibly digging. Were they here, digging for him?

Panic surged, which was the worst thing because the air was so thin, and his body awakened, his chest tightening and his lungs fighting to feed his failing system. Would they make it? Would he survive? The sounds were becoming clearer. Two voices. Shouting. So much shouting, voices becoming distinct – Tom and Tiff.

All his muscles cramped from lack of oxygen, his eyes burning so much he was sure they were bulging out of their sockets. He was out of time.

His head filled with dizzy thoughts. The six hours felt like an eternity. Bile filled his throat, forcing him to cough it out, gasping to catch a breath that wasn't available. The colours of his darkness spun and he began to sink into a deeper, darker realm – all his senses spiralling into its depths. As he fell, spinning like a leaf in October, a tune played softly around him – the voices of a thousand people singing with great passion:

I'm forever blowing bubbles, pretty bubbles in the air...

He smiled as Daniel's face appeared, looking happy as he held out his hand.

They fly so high, nearly reach the sky...

Richard held his own hand out.

Then like my dreams, they fade and die...

He couldn't connect. Daniel stood smiling, waiting.

Fortunes always hiding, I've looked everywhere...

He scrambled to grab hold of his son's hand.

I'm forever blowing bubbles, pretty bubbles in the air...

With one last effort, he dived forward and caught the boy's hand. As soon as they touched, air filled his lungs and he coughed and gasped. Daylight crashed in and two blurry figures loomed over him. Before he knew what was happening, he was hauled up and out by both arms.

The light blinded him but he was almost sure it was Tom and Tiffany gripping his arms. When he was clear of the grave, all three collapsed on the ground, their breaths loud and rasping.

"You alright, buddy?" Tom asked, the knife glinting in his hand, the blade now worn and chipped from prying loose nails – an implement of death turned into a lifesaver.

"I'm alive. I think." He coughed out while staring up at the overcast sky. The sun was doing its best to break through, but failing.

"Good, 'cause we aren't done yet." Tom sat up and patted Richard's chest. "No, we aren't done yet, mate."

Richard couldn't even begin to hazard a guess at what he meant. His mind raced as he tried to piece together all that had happened, including memories of his family darting around behind his eyes. If he had the energy, he'd punch Tom, but he wasn't sure if he'd done that already. Instead, he lay still and took a deep steadying breath. "What's next?"

"We found it, Richard," Tiff said, with an eagerness he hadn't heard in her before. He didn't reply but gave her a nod to continue.

"We found the control tower. We know where it is. It's were Block Eighteen is operated from. Charles is waiting for us."

Tom bent beside Richard and gripped his wrist, his hold warm against Richard's clammy skin. "It's time to end this shit, mate. We know where they are and we're going there now to take them fuckers out."

"How?" Richard pushed himself up to a sitting position. "I've been to the tower. It's got armed brutes and high fencing with barbwire. Without an arsenal, there's nothing a few starved and exhausted people could do against them."

"We'll cross that bridge when we get to it, mate. We're done with these objectives, this place, and that psychopathic tin-can bastard."

Richard didn't disagree. He wanted out as much as the rest of them did, and supposed it was better to die trying instead of living like a lab rat for the entertainment of their bloodthirsty audience.

It took the trio over an hour to arrive at the vantage point at the edge of the treeline. On the way, they filled each other in on the most recent losses, though Richard thought better of revealing the details of Ian's horrific death. Charles was waiting for them, his old face lighting up when they appeared.

"Richard, my dear boy. It's great to see you." He issued a fatherly hug.

Richard squeezed back, then turned his attention to the control compound. It was the one, there was no doubt about it, where Ian had met his agonising end. This time, however, it looked deserted, apart from trails of smoke rising from the far side. At the end of the dirt track the gates were open, but the pick-up truck was missing and the pool appeared to be drained.

"Well, chaps," Charles said, his shoulders down and his eyes sad, "it's just us four now. Our fallen campmates would want us to do this for them. They would—"

"Shut up, Chucky. The place is filled with cameras, microphones, and fuck knows what else."

"What's with the smoke?" Tiff asked.

"Your guess is as good as mine," Richard answered. "Nothing about this would surprise me anymore."

They hunkered in silence, watching – waiting.

The air chilled and the dull clouds released a shower over them – something of a relief after spending almost six hours in a grave. He looked around to assess their chances. Other than himself and Tom, in bad enough shape as they were, the other two looked physically wrecked. He cupped his hands and gathered enough rainwater to ease his parching thirst. Even the slightest replenishment would go a long away with the task before them.

Charles had a spark in his eyes – maybe hope – but lacked any real zip. Tiff was like a walking skeleton. Her taut skin revealed almost every bone in her body. She was clearly weak, and he wondered if a strong gust of wind would knock her over. Even so, he remembered how tough she'd been way back when they'd first awoken in the forest.

"Drink up," he said, "they know we're here. The path is clear for a reason." The others didn't reply. "I reckon we just walk in the front gate and take our chances."

"That's a suicide mission, mate," Tom said.

"What other option do we have?"

"Fuck it!" Tiff climbed to her feet. "Better to die trying then to continue like a goddam guinea pig. If we've learned anything from Carol's bravery, it's that we should go out on our own terms." She glared at the three of them, then walked out onto the dirt track, steam rising from her body in the light downpour. Then she nodded to the group and headed towards the gate.

The rest followed.

TWENTY-FOUR

As they approached the gate, the horror on the other side of the compound came into view, with participants from other blocks digging large rectangular-shaped holes in the dirt. Each was chained at the ankle to the next, like zombies, mindlessly slaving away without realising they were, in fact, creating their own resting place. Some holes were empty – cold, waiting for bodies – while others had already been filled and set alight. The stench of charred death rose into the air.

Tiffany turned away. "Oh my God..."

Tom shrugged. "Hey, at least we know where the smoke is coming from."

Richard stared at Tom and shook his head. The man just didn't know when to shut up. They walked along the gravel path, watching for guards but seeing none.

"Run!" Charles cried as an engine roared behind them. The pick-up truck was racing down the dirt track, its headlights flashing, horn beeping.

Richard and Tom sprinted forward and reached the gate first, but Charles and Tiff struggled as each tried to help the other.

The pick-up ground to a halt and two masked men hopped out. One of them opened fire on the gate, the rounds kicking up dirt as Richard and Tom ducked for cover.

The gunfire stopped and Charles and Tiff got up and broke for the gate, still a good thirty feet away. Two guard dogs were brought out from the back of the pick-up. One of the thugs held them on a long leash as he hyped them up.

"Run!" Richard roared, knowing with certainty what was going to happen. If they got the gate closed, they might have a chance. "Run!"

Charles stiffened and held his chest, then dropped in a heap in the middle of the dirt track.

Tiff cried out and ran back to him, but Richard could see the old man gasping and clutching at his chest.

"Charles? Charles!" she cried, looking from him to Richard and Tom, then back towards the masked men.

The dogs were released.

"Run!" Charles managed to shout.

Tiffany took off – the dogs heading straight for her. She pumped her arms as she sprinted for the gate.

Tom and Richard yelled encouragement, beckoning for her to get to them before the dogs reached her.

As she reached the gate, she gasped, her face almost purple, as if her chest was on the verge of explosion. She dived through the entrance and fell face first into the dirt. Richard and Tom slammed the gate shut behind her, and just in time, with the dogs smashing themselves against the chain-link, both in a frenzy.

"He's having a heart attack," Tiff cried between gaping breaths, turning over, almost begging the men to go help.

Richard could do nothing except watch as the masked men walked up the track. They stood over the dying old man, chatting to each other as if nothing was happening. Then one of them raised his rifle and, without hesitation, pulled the trigger.

"No!" Tiff screamed, erupting into tears at the sight of Charles' head bouncing from the impact – his blood and brains bursting onto the dirt.

The dogs howled but held their position.

With the men approaching, Richard and Tom grabbed Tiff and pulled her towards the control tower. The door at the main entrance was ajar and they stumbled inside, slamming it behind them.

"We don't have much time," Richard said as he tried to get through Tiff's hysteria. "They'll be in here any minute and they're going to kill us. We have to find the control room and try to call for help. It's got to be in this building."

The ground floor had a series of red doors running along a corridor in a straight line from the front door. Richard rushed forward and tried to open the closest one. Locked. He nodded to Tom to help him with the remaining doors. Every one they tried was locked. It was no use, until the last one at the end. With a loud click, the door opened outward. Richard signalled to the others, but was stopped in his tracks at the sight that met him. Bodies. Easily fifty to sixty of them, naked and in random piles, draped across each other. Some had fear engrained on their faces, while others stared at them with wide-open eyes. All the three of them could do was stare back with horror.

"It's a gas chamber," Tom said, pointing to the series of pipes and vents in the ceiling. "Come on, we haven't time to linger here. My guess is Control is up there." He pointed to a concrete staircase. "Come on!" he shouted, pulling Richard and Tiff away from the room.

The three of them struggled to ascend the stairs. Richard gasped for breath, his muscles aching all over.

Tiff sobbed, and he grabbed her around the waist and helped her along.

They reached the top and stood in a small foyer, with a door across from them, *Control Room* printed across it at head height.

"This is it," Tom said. "They must run the entire show from in there."

Shots rang out below and the wall splintered above their heads.

Everyone ducked behind the banisters. The gunfire stopped, and Richard couldn't believe it when the men downstairs started laughing. What the hell is going on?

"We're fucked," Tom said, his face panic-stricken. "They corralled us in here. And we fucking let them."

Richard wanted to take pleasure in Tom's anxiety, but more shots echoed up the stairwell and he focused his thoughts on the problem at hand. Perhaps Tom was right – getting to this point, it seemed, was all a bit too easy.

More shots thundered through the stairwell, followed by more laughter. When silence returned, the building's intercom system buzzed.

PARTICIPANT: SEVEN.

WE ARE DISAPPOINTED THAT YOU DECIDED TO TAKE THIS COURSE OF ACTION.

The Host's voice boomed through the foyer, the sound quality of the live transmissions much better than the set-up in Block 18.

HOWEVER...

WE ARE PLEASED THAT WE CAN NOW GET ON WITH THE FINAL OBJECTIVE.

REMINDER...

INFRACTIONS WILL NOT BE TOLERATED.

FAILURE TO COMPLY WILL RESULT IN PENALTY TO ALL EXTERNAL PLAYERS IN THIS GAME.

Richard straightened and shrugged. He knew exactly what The Host was on about, but didn't see the relevance in the current situation.

Tom looked up and mouthed – "*What is he talking about?*"

All the swirling memories in Richard's head coalesced into a definitive timeline, with Tom's face flashing across every visual. Then, as if on cue, one of the masked men tossed a handgun up the stairs.

The weapon landed at Richard's feet.

Tiff and Tom looked on with bewilderment as Richard reached down and picked it up.

The men below locked their rifles on him.

PARTICIPANT: SEVEN.

OBJECTIVE: YOU HAVE A CHOICE REGARDING… PARTICIPANT NINE.

VENGEANCE OR FORGIVENESS.

YOUR FUTURE AND YOUR FAMILY'S FUTURE DEPEND ON YOUR ACTIONS.

ALL SUBSCRIBERS ARE NOW LOGGED IN.

PROCEED.

Richard looked at the gun, then at Tom. The men downstairs laughed and he wondered what the hell was going on. *Is this happening? Is it a test? Has to be. The final test.* Did the subscribers want him to be a hero? Or get his head blown off and become a martyr? For who, though? Who the hell would see him as a martyr? Daniel and Elizabeth were dead. There was no-one else.

He looked at Tiff, who lay on the floor with tears streaming down her face, shaking her head at him – a signal for him not to do anything drastic?

True time disappeared as he grasped for rationale. His family were gone so what the hell was the point without them? Would they be alive now if Tom hadn't fucked Elizabeth? Impossible to know for sure. Nothing was going to stop the car from crashing that night.

Either way, it led him to this point. And The Host was in control. The man behind the speaker knew everything about them and wanted the trigger pulled so vengeance might be served. For the external players? Danny and Lizzy – manipulation for leverage. For viewers and betting, an act of wrath.

The foyer spun as blood drained from his head, his body racked by tremors. No, it had to stop, and he was the only one who could do it. Everything had been geared towards this moment. The Host wanted it all along. But in an act of defiance – a last-ditch effort to take back control – he removed his finger from the trigger and lowered the weapon.

"I'm not going to dance to your tune," he shouted. "I'm not doing this."

He shook stinging sweat out of his good eye and placed the barrel against the roof of his mouth. This was it. His son's cries resonated through his head. His small lifeless body lying motionless on the road. It was too much. Too fucking much. He applied pressure to the trigger, anticipating his release as the hot lead rocketed through his skull. Then the song played again, the same melody from within the coffin – a soundtrack that would shepherd him into the next world. Daniel had come to greet him – his hands out.

Richard looked at him. His poor son, taken so early, so unjustly. Elizabeth's searing words flooded back – all the lurid details: the nights away, the constant betrayal. He thought his heart would explode into his head as the horror of the accident replayed, over and over, her words and Daniel's cries echoing through his brain.

Then he opened his eyes.

Tom was standing in front of him, pleading for him not to do it. As soon as Richard locked eyes on him, rage gripped every sinew, every nerve, every aspect of his being. He pulled the gun from his mouth and pointed it at Tom.

In shock, Tom held out the knife and dropped it, his hands gesturing for understanding at it clanged off the concrete floor. "What are you doing, mate?" His eyes widened.

Richard pressed the muzzle against Tom's forehead. "You fucked my Lizzy. It's your fault they're dead."

Tom's eyes widened even more. "What? I haven't got a fucking clue what you're on about, mate."

"Yes, you do. You were fucking her and she was going to leave me for you, and that's why they are dead. Don't lie to me. Don't you dare lie to me!"

Tom held his hands up, sweat beading over his brows. "Richie, mate, they're messing with your head. None of that shit is true." He licked his lips, his gaze constantly shifting from the gun barrel to Richard's eyes. "We... We all have corrupt memories. Don't you get it? They can feed us any crap about before we got here and we'd probably believe it. They've been doing it since the beginning. Uploading and taking away whatever they want."

Richard shook so hard he thought he'd drop the gun. But he didn't. Tears brimmed and ran down his face. Were his memories true? How could he be sure? He couldn't even remember his last name.

With a deep breath, he took a step back, not sure what was true anymore. Were they being manipulated? Then a visual of Daniel, lifeless on the roadside, flashed behind his eyes, the boy's empty gaze connecting with his under the flashing blue lights as paramedics struggled to revive him.

It was real. It had to be. More real than where he stood now, pointing a gun at the man who'd driven the wedge between husband and wife, forcing his family from him. He squeezed the trigger. The hammer clicked, the sound drawn out, as if in slow motion. The gun kicked and the bullet cut through the air, and before he could comprehend his actions, Tom hit the floor, leaving a misty red bloom where his head had been.

Tiff screamed.

The men opened fire from below, dragging Richard out of his fugue. He dropped the weapon, grabbed Tiff's wrist and yanked her to her feet, surprised at his sudden surge of strength. She looked at him in horror. Brickwork splintered around their heads as bullets ricocheted through the foyer. He kicked the control-room door open and dragged Tiff inside with him.

All sound of gunfire disappeared when the door slammed shut. The room was a glowing white, and all he could hear was a faint buzzing coming from an unknown source. More static? Another speaker? It increased in volume and soon became overbearing, filling his head to such an extent he couldn't hear or see a thing.

"Tiffany?"

But she was gone. Vanished.

Everything was white. In every direction. No up or down. No gravity. No sense of weight. Nothing, just the sound bearing in on him from every point, growing louder with every passing second. Only there was no point, no connection – and then, in a flash, everything flipped from white to black.

TWENTY-FIVE

Hushed voices filled the shadows beyond his blurred vision. He felt alive, but aurally only. His mind was engaged in a desperate attempt to re-sync with his body, but there was nothing to connect with. The voices became clearer – a man speaking, his tone and inflections familiar. The more he blinked, the better his vision became, in both eyes – the darkness ebbing as light filtered in.

White.

He blinked a few more times. A room. A white room that smelled clinical – sterilised. Long fluorescent lights ran across the dank ceiling, casting a stark glow. Two figures stood within sight, off to his side. He couldn't move to get a better look. White coats. Their faces covered with white masks. All he could make out were their eyes – a man and a woman, staring down at him, analysing.

When he followed their gaze, he became aware of his body, naked and laid out on a dulled-grey table. Cold steel. He tried to move his arms, but realised thick black restraints held him down, with one across his chest. His mouth was moving, as if he was speaking, but no words came out, or none that he heard.

The man leaned closer. "Hello, Richard."

The girl didn't speak, typing instead at a furious pace on a silver pad in her hand.

The room spun as his mind struggled to cope. His vision went in and out of focus, his surroundings looming at one moment, then almost disappearing into the distance. The wall to his left was tiled in a dull cream. Then he realised his trolley was one of several in some sort of ward. He could barely make them out, but working on his peripheral vision, he saw that his was the only one occupied.

"What the fuck is happening?" he screamed, or thought he did, but again no sound came. He struggled against his bonds, to no avail – the straps didn't budge. *What the hell is going on? Where am I?* He tried to move his head again, but something tugged at the back of skull. Something tight – strong. He held his breath and pulled his head forward, but nothing happened other than the feeling of his skull splitting.

"I wouldn't do that, Richard," the woman said, her voice soft. "You'll hurt yourself."

She stepped into view and wiped his face with a damp towel, then fiddled with whatever was holding his head down. "Stay still, please. It'll take you a while to fully come back to us."

"What? Come back? What's happening?"

"You were logged into Block Eighteen for a long time. Disorientation is normal afterwards. Try to relax, please."

"You can hear me?" His heart surged. "Can you hear me?"

"Good, you're returning," the man said, "but if you keep struggling, I will have to administer a sedative. I don't want you to break the link while your results are still compiling."

Then it came to him, like the proverbial lightbulb flashing, the shock of realisation rushing through is body. "You're him. Aren't you? The Host?"

The man's eyes crinkled at the corners and he looked back at his tablet. Something about those eyes... Something so familiar... The man wore a black head-set with a mic arm extending from one ear to the side of his mouth. He spoke in another language – recording notes.

"Tell me. Please. Are you him?"

"Give it time, Richard. Your mind will reset. But before that happens, I must congratulate you on being the only participant to return to us."

"What am I, some kind of fucking lab rat?" He looked up at the man – The Host. "Let me go!"

The man didn't respond, continuing to make notes. The woman joined him, whispered in his ear, and the man looked down at him. "Okay, Richard, we would prefer if you were fully transitioned before continuing this assessment."

"What? Fuck you! Let me go."

The man nodded to the woman, who proceeded to insert a syringe into a port on Richard's arm.

He cried out in protest. Moments later his consciousness shifted, but he didn't go under, more like drifting in and out of a light doze. Even so, he was still aware of everything going on around him.

Then the room fell silent.

He struggled to stay awake – to hear what was being said.

"I must say, Richard, you must be very proud of what you achieved here. Your design is perfect, mate." The man removed his mask.

The sedative had taken hold – Richard could only watch on with helplessness. It had to be a dream? Surely. But it wasn't, as both Tom and Tiffany stood over him – healthy, his hair black, thick, and hers long, blonde, and both wide-eyed with excitement, as if they'd just discovered fire for the first time.

"Yeah, really good job, Richard," Tiff weighed in.

"With a few patches here and there," Tom continued, "Block Eighteen is going to be revolutionary, mate."

Richard's memory flooded back. Block 18 – that horrible place. It was his creation. Its purpose to rehabilitate criminals in a virtual-reality environment. It took him nearly two years to create and BETA test the platform, but he couldn't remember it ever going live.

"Tom, what did you do?" he mumbled. "Block Eighteen is not ready for human testing. We're months away from that?"

Tom shot Tiffany a look. "Go prep his room."

Tiffany, without hesitation, left the bedside and exited the ward.

"Relax, Richard. I'm leading the project now. Whatever comes after the stage you left it, is no longer any concern of yours." He smiled. "However, what matters now is what happens next. And I suppose it's great to have the original creator play a role in taking that next step."

Original creator? *I am the only creator.* Richard repeated this to himself as he scrambled for a clear and precise answer in the back of his mind. Everything was there, and it came to him: his most recent address, even his job title – Lead Design Engineer – he clenched his hands into fists and strained against his bonds. The heart monitor beside his bed beeped as if it was going out of control.

"And how about that Tiff one, mate? She played a fantastic role in today's session, didn't she? Not bad for an intern, eh? Girl should ditch the junior-designer career path and be a professional actor."

Tiffany. Tom was right, she was an intern. She'd come across excellent in her interview. A smart girl with an abundance of knowledge about the tech industry. He hadn't hesitated in bringing her onto his development team. Little did he know her capabilities went beyond technical troubleshooting – she was worthy of an Oscar after that session in Block 18.

Tom checked the monitors, reached in behind Richard's head, and released whatever was plugged into the back of his skull. "All done, mate." His mouth lifted at one corner. "I really enjoyed that session."

A strange sensation rushed through Richard's body. He figured it was similar to how astronauts felt returning home after a long period in space.

The doors opened and Tiffany returned with a wheelchair, followed by two orderlies. Richard's limp body was hoisted from the bed into the chair. His urge to fight was strong, but his body was non-responsive.

With his mind now clear, everything came to him – frame after frame – scene upon scene. It was all too much to process, especially when the darkest moment in his life came back to him.

Emotion filled his chest and surged into his throat, and tears ran freely as sobs erupted, his shoulders shaking beyond control.

The day after the car crash had been a cold and frosty winter's morning. He'd learned of the affair, if it could be called that after having gone on for so long. Years. It was basically a secret marriage. And with Tom of all people? *The betraying bastard. First he stole my wife and now the bastard is stealing my life's work.*

He'd given Lizzy everything. All he had. His life. His love.

On that brisk December day, with Daniel gone, he'd decided an axe from the shed would be the instrument of choice to quench his vengeance. What came after, including his trial, went by in a blur. He hadn't spoken a word since they'd found him in his snow-covered garden, bloody axe in hand and the dismembered body of his wife scattered around him.

The incident made national and international news. The world was curious about a guy who by society's normal standards seemed to be straight up and successful. Some journalists referred to him as, *The Axeman,* while others printed silly headlines such as, *The Lumberjack of London.* But, out of all the media frenzy, only one tag stuck with him – the front-page article from the local paper that showed a split image of Daniel's body on the road and Richard kneeling in his front garden. Evil, hurt, sorrow and sadness all rolled into a tabloid-sized page with a caption reading: Weeping Season.

The authorities sent him for psychiatric assessment, and for reasons beyond him, the doctors decided to sign him up to a never-heard-of-before rehabilitation program – an experiment in which he had no choice but to participate. *His* rehabilitation program.

He never asked why he wasn't tried for murder, as he already knew the answer. His memory was crystal clear now. His actions made him the perfect candidate, and Tom knew how to work that in his favour.

The company they worked for funded the project. Block 18. A digital homage to his fascination with concentration camps and the number to his and Lizzy's first apartment – the same residence where he developed the ground-breaking platform – a brilliant piece of software where they could rehabilitate a person's mind through a series of tasks in a safe environment. Once complete, it was to be the making of all of them. He'd never have to work another day in his life again.

It was all too much to process. Everything physical and mental was becoming too heavy and a numbness overtook him. In a state of shock, all he could do was watch as his limp and naked body was wheeled down a grey corridor. To his left were steel doors. All closed. On his right, tall windows provided a fleeting glimpse of snow-covered trees. He knew the facility was a long way from the United Kingdom, and his gut told him that wherever he was in the world, getting home was never going to happen.

Tom walked ahead and opened a door at the end of the corridor. "This is him."

Richard was lifted out of the wheelchair and thrown to the freezing floor. One of the orderlies followed him in and threw an old, grey blanket on top of him. A light came on, harsh and high, revealing dirt-covered concrete walls, looming, cold, and unforgiving.

The man then left.

"Don't worry, Richard," Tom said, standing in the doorway, "if things go right, we may try again tomorrow. You see, for murderous people like you and the rest of the participants, when given the choice, you all did one of three things. One, you were mentality weak for rehabilitation. Two, you opted to take the easy way out. Or three, and this applies to you, Richard, you reoffended. Fuck, mate, I even gave you a chance in today's session, and what did you do? That's right, you put a bullet in my head."

Richard groaned as the visual flashed behind his eyes.

"Now, I know you know what that means in Block Eighteen. Ha, you designed it that way, didn't you? On your recommendation, you wanted reoffenders to be given the death penalty. Do you remember discussing that one at the board meetings a few times? I used to love sitting back and watching their reactions to your ideas. Outlandish, but brilliant."

Richard lay motionless, trying to wrap his mind around everything. "Tom, please." He muttered, "I'm sorry... I really am. Please—"

"Begging was never your style," Tom said. "But, I've changed that stipulation. Just for you. You see, the entire project got shut down after what you did back in London. The bad press turned all of our major investors away. It took an incredible amount of effort and a lot of money on my part to get it going again. And here on Lyakhovsky Islands, we are allowed to operate without regulations."

Richard struggled up to his knees, the blanket falling behind him and he recalled the image he saw from outside the window. Beyond the glass, a baron winter wilderness. He frowned at the realisation of his situation – Tom made a deal with the Russians. *The crafty son of a bitch!*

"These islands are also known as The Ghost Lands. Did you know that? Well, that is all you are now, Richie. Well, at least to the real world. Nothing more than an apparition. So, I am continuing your work, mate, with an eager bunch of supporters who want nothing more than to see the project become a success."

Tom pulled a pack of smokes from his trouser pocket. He lit one up, exhaling slowly. "Oh, and one last thing. Elizabeth may have been your wife, but I loved her more than you'll ever know. She was my everything, and you took her away from me. I'll miss working with you, mate, but I'm going to enjoy plugging you back into Block Eighteen every day for the rest of your miserable life. It is what my Lizzy would have wanted and it is what you deserve."

The light flickered as the walls closed in. Richard watched as the cell door slammed shut and, with it, he was nothing more than a man reduced to hysterical screams. He dropped to the ground, pressing his cheek against the cold floor and what was left of his world turned to darkness.

THE END

ACKNOWLEGEMENTS

When I started writing the story that would eventually become this book, I lived in a two-bed apartment in Swords. I loved that rental and at the time, it was home to my new born son and wife to be, but it was also a place where I was able to really focus on my writing and turn some of my ideas into actual books – This book was wrote in that apartment.

I'll be honest, when I completed the first draft, I didn't really like the manuscript. However, somewhere along the line, the characters came to life and before I knew it, I had to turn the work in progress into an actual book. And with a newfound enthusiasm for Richard's story, I have to thank my editor, Eamon O Cleirigh, because without his expertise and encouragement, this book simply would not exist.

As with any novel, the completed work could not be achieved without a dedicated BETA reader team. I was lucky enough to have an eager bunch of readers who put this work through its paces. A big thank you goes out to those who helped me sculpt the final version – Lydia Capuano, Anna Hayward and Luke Newnes. Without you guys taking the time to read, compile notes and share your thoughts, I wouldn't have reached the finish line.

I think it goes without saying that dark/horror/weird fiction is going through a big resurgence right now with the likes of Stephen King still flying the flag and knocking out two to three books a year and his back catalogue getting turned into TV shows every few months – I feel fortunate that my work is alive during this time and without the support of my fellow writers, I wouldn't have any books in existence right now. With that in mind, I have to extend my thanks to Tim Lebbon and Adam Nevill for their friendship, experience sharing and above all, for allowing me access to their endless pits of advice.

Honourable mentions go to my creative colleagues; Kealan Patrick Burke, Matt Hayward, Barry Keegan, David Merriman, Mike Griffin, Ted Grau, Alex Knudson, Charlotte Zang, Mary SanGiovanni, Sadie Hartmann, Michael Patrick Hicks, Chad Lutzke, Peter Rawlik, Philip Fracassi,

Mike Davis and the rest of the Lovecraft eZine crew.

For the epigraph, I'd like to thank Devin Holt from the band *Pallbearer* and Patrick Walker from the band *Warning* for their inspiring music which has and continues to play a major role in my creative efforts.

To the people who matter the most, that's YOU – the one holding this book – the reader! Thank you for the gifts of your time and attention.

They say you should never judge a book by its cover... But I often do. And that is because I believe that one's work should be presented in the best possible way. The reader is owed that much. I can't thank Kenneth W. Cain and Boz Mugabe enough for the incredible job they have done with the typesetting and artwork for this novel. Thank you!

To my parents – whom this book is dedicated – Raymond and Sandra, thank you for always supporting my creative endeavours and for providing me with a home full of love and free thinking. And to my sister, Sinéad, and her husband, Alan, thank you for always being there for me.

And a final, heartfelt thanks goes to my darling wife, Orla and my son, Samuel. You both give me the strength to pursue my dreams and allow me to experience real love – I am eternally grateful to have you both in my life and I promise to keep trying to be the best husband and father I can possibly be.

ABOUT THE AUTHOR

SEÁN O'CONNOR grew up at the foot of the Dublin Mountains. From a young age he became fascinated with fiction, particularly stories based on the supernatural, horror, and the darker side of the human psyche. He currently resides in Swords, Co. Dublin, with his wife and son, where he is at work on his next tale of woe.

WWW.SEANOCONNOR.ORG

Printed in Poland
by Amazon Fulfillment
Poland Sp. z o.o., Wrocław